Where the Truth Lies

First Edition

Published by
Roscoe, Wilmott, Boothman & Associates

Where The Truth Lies

Valerie Boothman

Chapter 1

"The cottage rests on a magical garden bluff beside a natural water course with lush plantings of tropical trees. Its elevated location lends a cool "tree house" feeling with its garden setting surrounded by shady trees and flowering plants - gardenia, frangipani, tamarind, mahogany, palm and fern. Steps lead from the cottage doorway down through the garden to the breathtaking sandy white beach and pristine turquoise waters of the Caribbean Sea."

This was the description of Tamarind Cottage from the Estate Agents when Ben and Lucy were looking for a small house to buy in Barbados. When they saw it they liked the spacious wrap-around verandah on three sides of the property. The old coral stone walls, pickled timbers and open plan areas gave the cottage a beach house feel. They stopped looking at other properties when they found Tamarind.

Lucy had been shopping in Holetown. She pulled off the highway and parked the car behind Tamarind by the Frangipani trees taking in their sweet scent as she gathered her shopping and locked the car. She struggled to open the door of the cottage without putting down her parcels but managed it. She dumped the shopping heavily on the kitchen work top and kicked off her sandals. She crossed the tiled floor and opened the doors to the verandah. "That's better" she said to herself as sunlight flooded into the room. She put away the food she had bought and placed the bottle of Gordons in the drinks cabinet. "It's a bit early" she mused dispensing with the thought of a Gin and Tonic. She climbed the four steps to her bedroom, then undressed and stepped into the shower. She loved to feel the pressure of the water on the top of her spine and shrugged her shoulders. All the problems she had been dwelling on during the day were washed away, for a while.

She dressed in a white tee shirt and a pair of old denim shorts and brushed her hair leaving it damp. There was still enough heat in the day to dry it. "Oh sod it" she thought as she looked at her watch and realised it would be another half hour before the sun would set. She strolled into the kitchen and reached for a tall slim glass with a heavy base. "I was out of gin Ben" she said aloud to a husband who had been dead for six months. "I know" she said "you can forget the bread but never be out of gin. I've let you down there sweetheart" but she smiled as she remembered his words. She cut a slice of lime and added it to the ice cubes and then slowly poured the tonic water into the glass listening to the fizz and watching the bubbles climb up the sides. She stopped pouring, leaving an inch so she could shake the glass gently without spilling and listen to the noise the ice cubes made clinking against the glass.

Lucy slowly walked towards the CD player and pressed 'play'. She enjoyed a Gin and Tonic with Gary Barlow most evenings! She turned the sound of the music down a little so that it would not invade her thoughts. She walked through to the verandah and sat on her old swing chair and lowered her head to see the waves of the sea through the branches of the Mahogany tree. "It is true" she said aloud "it is like living in a tree house". She looked down into the garden and could see the narrow path which led to the beach. She had been too busy today to go for a swim or walk along the shore. Lucy pushed her feet against the cool timbers of the verandah floor causing her chair to gently move to and fro. She looked down at her long brown legs and thought "not too bad for 67" then laughed as she remembered the fine blue traces of varicose veins which had started to appear when she walked. Ben always told her she had super legs. He wouldn't have noticed the blue veins. She sipped her drink making a long sound of "ahhh" after the bitter sweet liquid trickled down her throat. She decided not to hurry it, she only allowed herself two G&Ts per evening and she had started early tonight.

She knew that she could not stay at Tamarind for ever. They had always agreed that when one died the other would return to their house in Somerset. Currently it was let but the tenants had been promised two months notice should either Lucy or Ben decide to go home. "Home" she said. "Where is home?" Here in Barbados where they had spent so many holidays and then bought this house when Ben had taken early retirement. Eventually they had decided to live here. She never understood why even after her father died her mother refused to visit them. It had been very strange, Barbados had been one of those subjects which as a child she knew was out of bounds.

Children can sense somehow that a subject is taboo. She remembered a school friend who had told her that she thought her parents had never married. "Why didn't you ask them?" Lucy had asked. Her friend had said "No I just knew it would have embarrassed them. I knew somehow that questioning her would have hurt my mother but there were clues". "What clues?" Lucy had asked. Her friend said "No wedding photographs and no anniversary celebrations". "I see" said Lucy still not quite understanding why no questions had been asked but then this was in an age when most couples who had children were married, unlike today.

It had been the same for her in some ways. There had been whispers when she was a child. It had infuriated her that she didn't know what they were talking about. She was sure the subject was about somewhere overseas and could not understand why it was such a secret. She remembered the look on her mothers face when she and Ben had first told her parents that they were going to Barbados for their next holiday, "what's the matter?" she had asked her mother and her father had quickly tried to cover up the problem and said "Oh that's wonderful darling lots of rum punches and Caribbean sun". Somehow she knew that the mysterious conversations she had never been privy to in her childhood were connected with her mothers response. She had also known there would be no point it pursuing it.

"Time for another" Lucy said aloud as she looked at her empty glass. She pressed 'play' again on her CD player. She threw the used slice of lime into the kitchen bin and cut another. Limes conveniently grew just outside her kitchen window. This time she was a little more generous with the gin and smiled to herself. She returned to the verandah and as she swung to and fro listened to the deafening love song of the cicada. You could time your watch by the insect's chorus. The sun was now dipping over the edge of the horizon creating shimmering lights of orange and yellow on the sea. It would very soon be totally dark. She could hear laughter coming from a party at the house next door. Her neighbour's house was a large modern square house owned by a wealthy glamorous socialite with palm trees in huge tubs on the patio and a massive swimming pool. They didn't mix in the same circles. The lady had just divorced husband number four and had benefitted very well financially at each break-up. When she and Lucy bumped into each other they would exchange "Hi" and smile but no more. Lucy was happy with that. She shivered although she wasn't cold. The sun had now slipped away over the edge of the horizon. She decided to go inside and close up the verandah for the night.

The phone rang, that funny ring that phones only make in Barbados. She decided not to answer and then she heard her friend's voice on the answering service. "Come on Luce pick it up it's only me" the gentle voice of Carrie could be heard. She picked up the phone "Hi Carrie, I was just closing up for the night that's all". "Want some company?" asked Carrie. "No not tonight but thanks. I am going to do some work on the computer then I will phone Rob and have an early night" said Lucy. "Well pop in for a drink tomorrow. Make it late morning and stay for lunch eh?" said Carrie. "Probably" said Lucy trying to leave the arrangement open. "See you about 11 then. Sleep well" Carrie seemed adamant.

She had planned to phone her son Rob who lived in Australia but it would keep, she thought. She completed closing up the verandah leaving the outside lights on for safety and locked her doors. She hadn't quite finished the G&T so picked it up and went over to her computer. She looked at the screen in front of her "Now just how are you going to help me?" Lucy asked. She wondered if creating her family tree would bring any answers. Was that the first step to take? Was their a connection between her ancestors and Barbados? How could she make plans to leave Barbados without knowing why their living on the island had made her parents unhappy. Why hadn't she thought about it before? Well she had, but it had always been something she was going to do and had never seriously started it. She had suggested to Ben that they looked into it but he had always laughed it off and said she was imagining it. That hadn't helped but she knew. What did she know? Well there was something, something she now had time to explore. The strange thing was that she had never discussed it with anyone other than Ben and he had been dismissive.

When her son Rob asked if she had put Tamarind on the market yet, she hadn't explained that she had no intention of leaving the island until she had solved her family mystery. She always told him there was no hurry and left it at that. He thought she was still grieving for Ben. Well she would always grieve for Ben but that wasn't it. Even Carrie who was a very dear friend and had been born on the island, knew nothing of this mystery. Lucy felt it was a very private matter.

She stared at the computer. "I am not in the mood to start again tonight Ben" she said. She enjoyed talking to him, even though he wasn't there. She wondered how long she would continue to do this. She never felt alone in the house as long as she could chat to him. She picked up her glass and moved to a large comfortable armchair covered in Sanderson chintz, switched on the TV and cuddled into the chair tucking her feet under her. Lucy drained the last drops of her drink. Although she was watching a programme her mind was elsewhere. She closed her eyes. She was over at Cattlewash Beach walking along the edge of the sea with Ben.

Chapter 2
1919

Adam Robert Richards sat in his study. He and his wife lived in a large house in the centre of Plymouth. He was a wealthy man involved in exports and imports but during the first World War had needed to diversify with a high degree of success. Now in the summer of 1919 the country was struggling to recover from a horrendous war which had cost millions of lives. Although he was now a very wealthy man he had great sorrow in his life for he had lost two sons, killed in France. His third son Edward had been discharged from the army in 1918 and after a long spell in hospital was now living in Newton Ferrers with his young wife. Newton Ferrers in Devon, is a small village some six miles south east of Plymouth on the River Yealm estuary. The Royal National Lifeboat Institution established a lifeboat station at the mouth of the Newton Creek in 1878 and a stone boat house had been built with a slipway into the River Yealm. Edward and his wife Charlotte lived not far from the boat house in a pretty cottage once owned by a relative of Charlotte.

Adam looked down at the documents on his desk which he had spent the morning mulling over. He knew that Edward was still unwell. Last winter he had suffered and Adam had been wondering if he could persuade his son and his wife to winter abroad if he could arrange that. Many of the Steam Packet Ships had been converted into troop ships during the war leaving limited transportation of His Majesty's Mail to parts of the Empire. Now they were being re-furbished and trade was growing slowly across the Atlantic. He examined the documents before him which had only arrived that morning. His old friend Stephen Drayton was now a Medical Practitioner based in Barbados and the letter from him advised James that he could arrange for Edward and Charlotte to winter in Barbados. He assured him that The Marine Hotel in Hastings, Barbados, had 200 rooms and there would be many people staying there during the 1919/1920 winter.

The Royal Mail Steam Packet Ships had returned to service now offering a twice monthly crossing from Southampton. Their first port of call was Cherbourg in France and then they crossed the Atlantic to Barbados as their first stop in the Caribbean, The journey would take approximately two weeks and if he could persuade them to leave England in late summer the crossing should not be too rough for Edward. James Robert stood up and walked over to the window. The last thing he wanted was for Edward to go away but Edwards future was probably dependant on him recovering good health. He knew that Charlotte found life difficult, Edward was not the man she married but she was a good soul and would always love and care for him. The break would be good for them both. He was reluctant to tell his wife of his plans. Emily would not accept that there was anything wrong with Edward. She just kept saying that it was taking time for him to recover from the war. She would be totally against James plans.

Adam had made his decision. The first person he must convince was Charlotte, without her agreement it would not happen. He had sent a message to her asking her to visit them and stay for lunch. He knew that with sufficient notice she could arrange for the Vicar's wife to stay with Edward whilst she was away. The daily coach from her village would arrive in Plymouth at 11 am and this would allow them time to discuss the matter before lunch. She would return on the 3 pm coach to Newton Ferrers. He had had to find an excuse for her visit. Due to Edward's illness Adam had been granted power of attorney for his son's finances and consequently had occasionally involved Charlotte in meetings. She was then able to explain to Edward any changes in their financial circumstances. This was used as a reason for her visit. He looked out of his study window. It had been very cloudy in the early morning but the day was looking brighter and he hoped it would be fine for Charlotte. He looked at his watch and put it back in his waistcoat pocket. She should be here very soon, he had sent his man to meet her and accompany her to the house. His wife Emily had been asked to arrange a light lunch but the meeting would take place first.

Charlotte awoke and immediately listened for any noise as she had done since they first came to live at the cottage. A reception room downstairs had been converted into a bedroom for Edward and the builders had been able to convert an adjoining outhouse into bathroom facilities for him. She had had an undisturbed night and felt refreshed from it but immediately worried that Edward may have needed her and she had not heard him. She quickly put on her wrap and descended the stairs. His door squeaked at the hinges as she quietly pressed the latch and opened the door. It was a pretty room with blue and white curtains at the windows and a pale cream carpet. The walls of the cottage were thick and each of the two windows had window seats with cushions covered in the same material as the curtains.

As she crept quietly towards his bed he turned and smiled at her. She kissed his brow and then sat on the side of the bed. "A good night?" she asked. "I think so" he answered "I don't remember any problems". Charlotte left the room and pulled her wrap close round her as she walked into the kitchen to make two cups of tea. She prepared a tray with her fine blue and white china and when she heard the whistle of the kettle she poured the boiling water into the tea pot. She used the tea strainer so that no tea leaves could escape and then carried the tray into Edward's bedroom. He was then sitting up in bed and eagerly took the cup and saucer from her. The sun was shining through the bedroom windows and you could hear the bird song in the garden

As Charlotte sipped her tea sitting on the side of the bed she knew she must explain to him that she would not be here during the day. She said "Edward darling, Mrs Patchet is coming to see you today". He immediately reacted to this news because he knew this meant that Charlotte would be away. "Why?" he demanded and frowned. "Well your Papa has asked me to attend a meeting in Plymouth so I must go and you know Mrs Patchet is wonderful with you". Edward looked at her "No don't go" he said "when did Papa ask you?". She answered "Edward, he sent a message a few days ago but as it upsets you I decided not to tell you until today." She rose and said "I must prepare" and closed the door behind her. By the time Mrs Patchet arrived she had helped Edward to wash and dress and he was sitting in his chair by the window. It was a lovely morning, some late primroses were dotted here and there on the grassy bank beneath the trees which bordered the lane. Most trees were in young leaf, that very bright green when buds turn to leaf. The sky had a blue haze of late spring and he watched her walk down the lane wearing a smart long brown skirt with matching jacket and a jaunty cream bonnet on her head.

He knew she would turn and wave before she reached the bend, and she knew he would be watching and waiting for her wave. As she climbed on board the coach she wondered why Papa needed to see her again. She turned and waved although she couldn't see him. The truth was she was quite looking forward to the trip to town. It was an escape from her daily life which was not always easy. When they married in 1914 Edward was a tall handsome athletic young man with a wonderful future ahead of him. His experiences in the war had changed all that but he was one of the lucky ones, he had come home albeit experiencing nightmares of which he couldn't speak.

The young man her father in law had sent to meet her was waiting as she alighted the coach. It was only a few minutes to walk to the town house and it was a fine early summer day. When she arrived she was taken into the sitting room to meet Edward's mother who greeted her warmly. "How is my precious boy today Charlotte?" she enquired. "Well he had a good nights rest and he ate two eggs for breakfast. We try to go for a short walk each day but he continues to feel the cold so I make sure he is always well wrapped up even on these lovely late Spring days Mama." Emily Richards smiled at her daughter in law and patted her arm "Edward chose well my dear" she said "now Papa is waiting for you in his study I have instructions not to keep you chatting. We can talk more at lunch."

Adam Richards turned his chair and rose to greet Charlotte and held both her hands in his. "Come and sit down my dear, are you well?" Charlotte nodded and smiled at the old man of whom she was very fond. "And how is Edward coming along, do you think he is getting better?" Charlotte thought how best to explain to her father in law how Edward was progressing. She didn't want to raise his hopes but needed to be very honest. "Well Papa we had a good night last night which we both required. The previous night was difficult, I heard Edward shouting and he was very distressed. He has nightmares as you know, and when I try to wake him from them he stares at me as though he doesn't know who I am. He talks to his old comrades as though they are there in front of him and sometimes he shouts so loudly I am glad our neighbours are not living next to us." Adam shook his head in worry "are you able to manage him or should we arrange for some help?" he asked. "No I don't need help at the moment and I will ask if I do. Actually these bad times are becoming fewer which I think gives me hope for our future" Charlotte said. "He is always cold, on a lovely sunny morning he will not let me leave the door ajar and the windows have to be closed. Last winter was not easy you remember he was nearly sent back to hospital. He wants the fire lit mid morning every day. I am so afraid he may catch a cold because he is not strong enough yet."

Adam looked round his office. The thick carpet, the oak panelled walls, the mahogany furniture and the paintings on the walls were proof of his successful business. He waved his hands around in the air "this was a business my three sons were to inherit" he said. "I looked forward to them taking the reins from me and in time there would be grandsons to take the business forward. Now fate has taken away two of my sons fighting for their country and my poor Edward is not well". Charlotte said quietly "many of our dreams will not come true but we have to make the most of the hand that has been dealt us." She wanted to add "and don't bank on grandchildren from my marriage."

Adam looked into her face and embraced her warmly. "You are wise beyond your years my dear and of course you are right. I am no longer worried about the future of this business, truly, I am now only concerned for what is best for you and Edward. You are a strong woman Charlotte and now I am going to test you even more. "She looked up at him quite alarmed and wondered what was coming next. " I have a plan" said her father in law. "Oh dear" said Charlotte "thinking what more do I have to take on board."

Chapter 3

Cattlewash had always been special. With eyes closed she could see them. They held hands like lovers as they splashed their feet amongst the waves. She lost awareness of the drama on the television. Her mind went back to happy days when she and Ben had thought they would live for ever. When they had purchased Tamarind Cottage they had been so excited. It was rather smaller than the house they had in mind but they liked the open plan arrangement of the sitting room, dining area and kitchen. The bedrooms were large and airy and both en-suite, with remote air conditioning and ceiling fans so ideal for visiting friends and family. Ben used to love sitting on the verandah watching the sun set. He used to swim most days and play golf once or twice a week and was never ill.

When Ben had died suddenly of a heart attack it had been a huge shock. There had been no warning of any heart problem. It had been so difficult for her to phone Rob in Perth and tell him. Alex, Rob's wife, had answered the phone and had wanted to chat but Lucy had said "Please get Rob Alex, it's bad news". Rob had taken it badly but he dropped everything and booked a flight to Barbados via Dubai and London, a flight which took him 32 hours. Three days after Ben's death Lucy set off from Tamarind to pick up Rob from Grantley Adams Airport in Bridgetown. Carrie and her husband Tom were very close friends and had wanted to meet him at the airport and bring him to Tamarind or at the very least go with her but she wanted to meet him alone.

As she left the house she felt quite composed. She turned

right on to Highway 2A and looked at her watch. "Plenty of time" she said aloud. As she approached Lawrence Johnson roundabout she remembered how she and Ben had always appreciated that the major roundabouts had been named after famous or important men in the history of Barbados. Soon she would approach D'Arcy Scott, then Everton Weeks, Clyde Walcott, etc., and then the roundabout where the Emancipation Monument stood. As she approached the Garfield Sobers roundabout she wondered if this could be adopted in England. Perhaps a Sir Ian Botham roundabout on the A5 or a Margaret Thatcher roundabout on the A10. Suddenly she realised that these thoughts had been disguising her real mood. Tears were streaming down her cheeks "Oh Ben" she said quietly.

She parked the car and put on her sunglasses and sun hat, it was very hot. She strolled over to 'Arrivals' and checked the incoming flights from London. It looked as though his plane had landed early and her heart skipped a beat. She walked around but could not bring herself to sit down on one of the benches. Lucy watched all the people coming through the airport, most of them white skinned and loaded with luggage. There were black and white Bajan, some returning home with just a cabin bag on wheels. All the porters were vying for the holiday makers business. They looked tired after a long flight but their faces showed anticipation of a holiday in the sun. Then she saw him, tall, dark hair lightened by the sun pulling a large soft holdall on wheels, wearing jeans and an open neck short sleeved blue shirt. He looked so like Ben. All Lucy's earlier composure flew out of the window. He saw her running towards him, let go of his suitcase and opened his arms, she ran into them clinging together in their grief.

No words were spoken for some minutes whilst they both pulled themselves together. Rob dumped his bag in the boot of the car and said "Shall I drive?" Lucy nodded. They made small talk on the forty minute journey home aware of how each one of them needed time before they could speak of Ben.

When they arrived at Tamarind Rob opened up the verandah doors allowing light to flood the house. It would soon be sun set and Lucy didn't know what to say. There was an awkward silence. Rob said "Mum I'm tired and hungry and will probably have an early night but I fancy a swim. Why don't you knock up something for us to eat whilst I quickly unpack and go for a dip?" Lucy was happy with that. She pretended not to watch as he ran down the steps and through the garden. She busied herself setting the table on the verandah and making a simple Bajan chicken salad.

After his swim Rob ran back up the steps and stood by the garden tap washing the sand off his feet. As he came through the door Lucy threw him a towel. When he had changed into shorts and a tee shirt he poured her a Gin and Tonic and took a beer out of the fridge. "Ah! Banks Beer" he said as he took his first swig. "Alex was sorry she couldn't come but it is difficult for her to leave her job at a moments notice and the children would be a problem too" said Rob "but she sends her love and said to tell you that you are in her thoughts" he added. "Oh Rob I never expected Alex to be able to come but it would have been wonderful to see her" said Lucy. They sat down at the table, suddenly neither of them very hungry, pushing food round their plates. Lucy decided to be brave and started to tell Rob about the plans for Ben's funeral. She told him she had chosen her favourite hymns for the service because she wasn't sure which Ben would have picked. "Dad would be fine with whatever you have arranged Mum" Rob said quietly. "I did know he wanted to be cremated" said Lucy. "Fine" Rob answered nodding his head slowly.

Carrie and Tom called the next morning just as Rob and Lucy were having breakfast. The birds were flying from the branches of the Mahogany trees on to the bar of the verandah and Rob was feeding them scraps. Lucy scolded him "you are making them too welcome. They can make such a mess". Rob smiled "nothing changes" he thought. Rob thanked Carrie and Tom for the tremendous support they had given his mother at this sad time but they shrugged their shoulders. Tom said "We would do anything for your parents. They were our best friends as you know".

The next few days had been difficult for Lucy and yet there were precious moments sitting on the verandah with Rob in the evening, sometimes joined by friends, when they spoke of Ben. Lucy found herself laughing when Tom related a time they had been trying to swim in the surf at Crane Beach and Ben had been bowled over several times before he could scramble up the beach away from the huge breakers. Then she suddenly stopped, feeling guilty that she was laughing. Carrie understood and quickly touched her arm "it's ok Lucy" she said, smiling at her and they both understood the moment.

The Funeral service was held at St John's Church on top of Mount Tabor in the parish of St John. The church was surrounded by trees and gravestones. A wide avenue of tall trees led from the car park to the door of the church. The shadows from the trees fell across the path creating stripes of dark and light. The inscriptions on the gravestones showed that many early English settlers had died from fever and disease hundreds of years ago. It was a simple service but the church was crowded with their friends and acquaintances. Rob had been a popular member at Royal Westmoreland Golf Club and his sudden death had been a great shock to everyone. Following the service, the cremation was a very private affair with only very close friends to support Lucy and Rob. Carrie and Tom had laid on refreshments and drinks at their house after the service but Lucy and Rob only stayed as long as seemed polite before escaping to the peace and quiet of Tamarind.

The day before Rob was due to fly home to Australia he and Lucy drove to the Funeral Directors to collect Ben's ashes. The man had asked Lucy if she required an elaborate urn but she quickly told him that a simple tin or a box would do. "Shall we put Dad on the back seat?" Rob asked her with a smile. "No I think I will let him sit on my lap" she replied smiling. Rob handed her the tin and she wrapped her arms round it and pulled it close to her chest. They set off driving up the hill to cross the island. They passed Farley Hill National Park and carried on down through St Andrews Parish, past the church towards the coast. The view of the East Coast with the Atlantic breakers pounding the shore was magnificent. So different to the Caribbean Sea and quiet shores on the West Coast. As they approached Barclays Park and the beach Rob asked Lucy to tell him where to stop. "Further yet" said Lucy quietly. Within a few minutes they were at Cattlewash Beach and Lucy said "Just here Rob please".

He pulled off the road. Lucy let her sandals fall into the foot well in the car and opened the door. "Would you like me to come with you?" asked Rob. "I think this is something I need to do on my own, but thanks " said Lucy.

She walked down the sandy path through the bushes towards the beach feeling the sand between her toes. It was a glorious sunny day and the wind was blowing strongly off the Atlantic Ocean. This was their favourite place. Cattlewash was the place to where they would regularly drive. The sea was too strong to risk swimming but they would examine the rock pools and walk along the edge of the sea dodging the breakers and looking out at huge white foam and inland up into the hills which had once been covered with sugar plantations and where you could sometimes find traces of where the old railway used to run.

This was a very unspoilt part of the island, no expensive restaurants, no commercialism, just a simple beach bar in the distance. "Oh Ben, there was still so much we had to do" whispered Lucy as she held the tin containing his ashes very tightly. "Oh Ben, Oh Ben" she whispered as tears ran down her cheeks. She remembered that when she took off the lid she must stand with her back to the wind so that the ashes would blow away from her. She recalled reading that the author and Lakeland Fell walker Alfred Wainwright had asked that his ashes be scattered over his favourite hill, Haystacks in Buttermere Valley in the Lake District. In one of his books he had added " and if dear reader, should you ever get a bit of grit in your boot as you are crossing Haystacks in years to come, please treat it with respect. It might be me." She smiled now and struggled as she tried to remove the lid "here we go Ben" she said. Suddenly it came loose and a swirl of ashes leapt into the air and were gone. "Bye Ben" she called into the wind.

Lucy turned and looked back along the beach. The breeze was blowing her hair around her head. Rob had left the car and was walking slowly towards her. "Ok Mum?" he enquired cautiously. Lucy nodded "lets go home". Rob drove slowly thinking how difficult it would be for his mother now with his father gone. They had been very close. His parents had lots of friends at the Golf Club and Lucy had played regularly but would she continue now? He hoped so. He wished he could persuade her to join him in Perth. Alex would like that and the children would get to know their grandmother but now was not the time to push for that. She needed time to grieve. Letting go of Ben's ashes had been therapeutic. Emotionally there was nothing else to do. They didn't speak as he slowly drove back to Tamarind. He turned left at Belleplaine and climbed the hill through Turners Hall Woods then back into St James and down towards the West Coast. When they arrived at Tamarind they found Carrie had left a note under the plant pot outside the door. The note just read "Come for supper - before sundown C "

Carrie and Tom lived inland in St Peter in a house that had once belonged to Carrie's parents. She had been an only child and she had inherited it when her parents died. It had once been a Plantation House with much history. Part of the house had been destroyed by fire years ago but most of it had been saved and you could not see any damage now. Bougainvillaea of several colours climbed the walls disguising the repairs. As suggested Rob and

Lucy drove to their friend's house in the late afternoon. They were all very relaxed and were able to talk about Ben comfortably. After a wonderful meal, Rob drove Lucy back to Tamarind. "You have good friends there" said Rob. "Yes I am very lucky" Lucy replied. Tamarind was in darkness, just the sound of the cicadas greeted them. "Our last night cap?" suggested Rob and Lucy was very happy to spend another hour sitting with Rob talking about his family and his hopes for the future. The next day Carrie collected them both and she drove to the airport. So much had happened since Rob had arrived nearly two weeks ago. Perhaps the healing had started, just a little. Rob promised to phone her as soon as he arrived home and then after big hugs was gone, striding away towards 'Departures'. Lucy and Carrie looked at each other and smiled knowing they were thinking the same thing, he had Ben's walk.

They both needed to buy groceries so called at Holetown on the way back and Carrie also needed fuel. When they arrived at Tamarind she didn't ask Lucy if she wanted company she just followed her into the house and made coffee whilst Lucy put away her purchases. They sat on the verandah together. "I know Rob thinks I should put Tamarind on the market and either join him and Alex and the boys in Perth or go back to England. I would have to give the Bennetts two months notice to leave our house in Charlton Musgrove. They've been good tenants and have been there about five years" said Lucy. Carrie stood up, moved her chair closer to Lucy's and patted her arm as she sat down. "No need to make any decisions for a long time Lucy" she said. Lucy nodded and appreciated Carrie's thoughtfulness. "Just phone me if you need me" added Carrie "whatever the time of day or night". Lucy nodded again. She daren't speak or she would start weeping again and there had been enough weeping in the last few weeks.

Lucy had relied heavily on both Carrie and Tom and other friends in the weeks that followed Bens death but slowly she started to lead a different life than she and Ben had lead. She decided she no longer needed Diana her maid who used to come to clean three times a week and would also cook for her dinner parties. There was just no need for her now and Diana understood, especially when Lucy gave her a cheque to compensate for two months loss of salary. Sometimes Diana would pop in with a coconut cake she had just made and they chatted about Diana's husband Cyril and her large family. Lucy now enjoyed getting up early before the heat of the day and cleaned the house when it needed it and then would go for a swim. "One person doesn't need a maid" she told herself.

Valerie Boothman

Chapter 4

Lucy opened her eyes and realised she had been far away. She turned off the television and decided to have an early night but first she read a few pages of the current book she was reading. She read most nights before turning off the light. Her family research could continue tomorrow she decided.

She rose early and went for a swim. She was not a strong swimmer but enjoyed swimming and would often wear goggles and a snorkel looking for brightly coloured fish darting about in shoals. Now the coral was dying due to pollution in the ocean and there was no sign of the Yellow Tail Damsel fish or the French Grunt or Blue Tang they used to see when they had first come to the island. So much coral had died which was their breeding ground. After swimming around for a while she lay back in the water trying to float and then laughed as a wave suddenly washed over her face. She chatted to a couple who were on holiday from the States who explained this was their last dip before catching their flight home later in the day. Apart from them the beach was deserted for miles. Back in the house she showered and dressed simply in shorts and a top. She looked over to her desk where the computer was beckoning her "ok you win" she said.

A few weeks after Ben's death she had joined Ancestry.co.uk and had started creating her family tree. She thought that was a good place to start. She would not call herself computer literate but neither was she computer illiterate she decided. She sort of bumbled along and if she was really stuck she would contact Rob even though he was in Australia. He used to amuse her by answering his phone saying "Tech Support" when he could see it was her telephone number on his i Phone. She had attended evening classes at Harrison College which had helped to improve her skills. "Right" she said aloud "password" then "enter". She had made a start calling herself the 'home person' so that every name she entered could be identified by their relationship to her for example 'second cousin by marriage' and that was helpful. She had entered Robs full name and his birth record and also the date of his marriage to Alex and their children's names and birth dates but she knew her challenge lay in the other direction. When Lucy's mother died the Solicitors had forwarded to her the family bible that had been passed down through generations. He said it contained several documents which had been placed there for safe keeping. There were a few birth, marriage, and death certificates, an odd newspaper cutting where a member of the family had written to the newspapers and many strange small receipts. She decided to see how far she could get creating her tree on Ancestry and then in the evening she could settle down with the Bible and see if there were any certificates buried among the pages which could help. It was amazing how quickly she built the tree. She knew the dates of birth of her parents and her grandparents and where it was easy to find their records she entered the facts at the same time. When she couldn't find the record she filled in details from her memory knowing she could always amend it later. There was something very emotional about entering that Lucy Barnes, born 1943 in Taunton, Somerset had in 1963 married Ben Harrison, born 1942 in Bristol. The sad part was when she entered Ben's death in Barbados in 2009 aged only 67 years.

To her knowledge her mother Susan was born Susan Louise Richards on 10th February 1920 in Plymouth, died 2001 aged 81 and her father John Robert Barnes was born on 9th November 1916 in Taunton and died in 1990 aged 74. Nan and Grandpa Richards had lived in Plymouth. She was amazed at how little she and knew about both sides of the family. Her fathers parents had also lived in Plymouth. She knew that Grandpa Barnes had been involved in shipping or exports. There were no brothers or sisters to ask for help. She was able to find the record of her fathers birth in Taunton Somerset but could find no record of her mothers birth. She could not understand this.

Lucy concentrated her memory more on her family rather than Ben's because that is where the mystery lay. She remembered Granny Richards very well. She used to stay with her during school holidays and Granny taught her how to make Fairy Cakes and Flapjacks. Grandpa Richards had never really recovered from injuries received during the First World War and died when Lucy was only seven so she didn't remember him very well. They had both doted on Susan their only daughter and consequently Lucy too was very special to them. John and Mary Barnes, her fathers parents were also very loving grandparents and Grandpa Barnes used to take her walks near to where they lived, through the fields to the stream and they would throw pooh sticks into the strong current. She would run along the side of the brook to see if they had reached 'Dead Mans Gully'. It had been good fun.

Chapter 5
1919

Adam spoke very slowly and clearly and stared at Charlotte as he started his deliberation. "I have heard of persons who are sick and unable to cope with the English winter. It is proven that if they winter in a warm sunny climate their health improves and when ready they can return to England and resume a normal life." Charlotte looked down at her hands which were shaking and she tried very hard to control them. Adam continued "I have an old friend who lives in Barbados, he has a medical practice there, his name is Stephen Drayton. He can arrange to receive you and Edward in Barbados before the winter starts. There are good hotels, should you prefer he will arrange for you to take a house. There will be servants and friends of the Draytons to support you. You will not be alone."

Charlotte could not hide her alarm "but the passage to Barbados, how long does it take, how long would we be at sea, would there be a doctor on board the ship if Edward needed one?" "The journey should take no more than two weeks and there would be an excellent Ships Doctor who cares for the passengers and crew." Adam answered.

Charlotte looked at Adam "I would not see my parents nor friends, nor you and Mama, I would be alone" she sobbed and covered her face with her hands. "My dear" said Adam "I am just asking you to think about this suggestion, no more, I cannot make you go and only you could persuade Edward." He continued "you would both be away for perhaps six months, more if you wished, less if you so wished, I am just asking you to consider it. Tell no-one, not even Edward until you have made the decision." "Does Mama know?" asked Charlotte. "No she believes Edward will get better soon, she is not a practical woman like you Charlotte. I will not tell her unless you decide to go, then I will have to face her anger. Dry your tears we must join Mama for lunch, give me your answer in seven days". "Oh seven days!" said Charlotte. "Yes there is much to arrange if you are to leave these shores in late August and it is important that the accommodation I will arrange for you in Barbados will be to your liking."

They walked together into the conservatory which had been built on to the back of the house overlooking the garden where it was pleasant to have informal lunch parties. Emily scolded Adam for keeping Charlotte to himself for so long and served home made chicken and ham pie with salads and cheese and chutney. At first Charlotte felt she couldn't eat at all but eventually she did and enjoyed it. Adam excused himself to attend to a caller and Emily tried to persuade Charlotte to take another helping. She confidentially whispered to Charlotte "come along have some more, are you eating for two yet?" and she winked knowingly in a womanly way. It was then that Charlotte realised how little her mother in law knew of the circumstances of her marriage. When Adam returned to the table he looked at Charlotte and said "is something wrong?" Emily's comments must have created a reaction which was shown on her face. "No no this is a lovely lunch, Edward would have enjoyed the pie." "Then there is plenty for you to take back with you my dear" said Emily.

The old Grandfather clock in the hall chimed and Adam said "I will walk with you to the coach my dear, mustn't be late." Charlotte kissed Emily on both cheeks and assured her that Edward would enjoy the pie that evening as Adam opened the heavy front door and they stepped out into the street. She linked arms with the old man in a familiar way, she had always liked him and he had always treated her as the daughter he had never had. He looked down at her and patted her arm, "I want only what is best for you both my dear" he said. She answered "I know Papa". There were tears in his eyes as he watched her board the coach and he lifted his hand to wave and then strode away down the street. They had arranged that in a weeks time he and Emily would visit them in Newton Ferrers. Sitting on the coach Charlotte watched the faces of other passengers but her mind was far away. Did she really want to go to Barbados?

As Charlotte walked up the lane towards the cottage she could see movement. The door opened and Edward came outside to meet her. He was leaning on his stick but he managed to wave long before she was in earshot. She knew he would have been waiting a long time and he was wearing a sweater and scarf which he must have donned well in advance of the expected time of her arrival. She could see him smiling and she smiled back and hurried up the hill towards him and embraced him. She could feel his bones through the sweater, he felt so slight and she was frightened of crushing him. Mrs Patchet said "Oh you are back then my dear, I couldn't get him to sit down he kept going outside to watch for you coming." "Everything alright Mrs Patchet?" asked Charlotte. "Just fine" she answered. They looked at each others faces and smiled knowingly, Mrs Patchet knew how much her time was appreciated. She would not take any money but Charlotte gave her half of the huge piece of pie Emily had sent and Mrs Patchet welcomed that. She put on her coat and said she would come anytime Charlotte needed her. Charlotte gave her a hug which spoke volumes.

Edward said "lets sit by the fire and you can tell me all about your visit, were my parents well? He bent forward and put a log on the fire. Charlotte said she had enjoyed a lovely lunch and showed him the pie and asked if he would like some. "Perhaps tomorrow" he said "but lets toast crumpets and have a cup of tea." Charlotte was content with that. "Oh Tim Greenwood the post man's boy dropped off some logs this morning, good name for a boy delivering logs I thought" and he chuckled at his joke. Charlotte laughed too, pleased to see him in such a good mood.

She brought out the long handled brass toasting fork and the crumpets and let Edward pierce the crumpet and hold the fork towards the flame. This was usually her job. She turned to put the kettle on and prepare the tea but suddenly she thought she could smell burning. She turned to look at Edward. He was staring into the flames with a frightened expression on his face. He let the fork fall to the hearth and he screamed as the crumpet caught fire. Then he put his face in his hands and sobbed and sobbed. Charlotte held him in her arms sitting on the arm of his chair and rocked him gently until the sobbing subsided. She then led him into his room and helped him to wash and get into his pyjamas. He clung to her and kissed her neck and told her he loved her, then climbed into bed and was asleep within a few minutes.

Valerie Boothman

Charlotte returned to the sitting room and sat by the fire. She picked up her needlework but then put it down, how could she concentrate on anything. She stared into the flames and wondered what Edward saw when he stared into the flames. What did his memory see? When would it end? She was nearly thirty years old and had such a huge decision to make. Did she want to leave Devon? No. Did she want to leave her family and friends? No. Would leaving England and starting a new life in Barbados, even if only for a few months or a year at the most, help Edward? Perhaps, but she didn't know.

This cottage had thick stone walls but winters were cold. Logs had to be carried through and stacked at each side of the fireplace and it wasn't a job Edward could do so it was always up to her. She tried to do it whilst he slept. Should they move into Plymouth? She didn't really want that either. Charlotte made a cup of tea and toasted a crumpet for herself, it was necessary for her to keep well and strong. She was exhausted so retired early to her bedroom. She lay in bed thinking of her husband in his room below. She thought of her mother in law's comments " are you eating for two" and she smiled at the irony of Emily's question. She thought of the passionate nights they enjoyed before he went off to be a soldier. Eventually she fell asleep.

The next morning Charlotte arose early and decided to stack the logs the boy had brought the previous day. She took her small wheelbarrow and put in as many as she could lift and wheeled it through the back porch into the sitting room. She then lifted each log and carefully stacked them in rows from left to right and at the end of each row started on the next row up. Suddenly she felt a hand on her shoulder which made her jump. It was Edward and he was dressed. He motioned her to sit in the chair and he started laying each log in rows on top of each other at each side of the fireplace.

He could only use one hand as the other was holding his stick to support him. When the wheelbarrow was empty he looked down at it. Charlotte started to stand up but he pushed her back into her chair. Edward walked outside and returned carrying two logs, the most he could carry. He carefully laid them in rows and then although limping and leaning on his stick returned to the pile outside and brought two more logs into the house. He continued this way although sweat was pouring off him and he was slowing down. Charlotte whispered "let me help Edward" but he shook his head and continued until each side of the fireplace was stacked with logs. He was covered in sawdust and twigs and his arms and hands were dirty and his face was white. He smiled at Charlotte and said "Man's work" and slumped down in his chair.

Charlotte threw her arms round him and wept openly at the same time saying "Well done darling, well done." He was exhausted and allowed her to tidy up all the dirt and twigs and she brought a basin and washed his face, arms and hands. He quickly fell asleep in the chair and she looked down at this man whom she deeply loved. What was best for him? When he stirred she made breakfast of scrambled eggs and a small slice of bacon and toast. They sat at their small kitchen table eating hungrily. Charlotte said "Edward what you did this morning stacking the logs was wonderful." He smiled and said nothing. She continued "but it is silly for you to do too much too soon. Now that we both know you can stack the logs then it is sensible that you help me and don't try to do it all on your own" she quickly corrected herself and said "I mean I will help you." He looked at her and agreed saying "yes you can help me" and they laughed together. It was such a small thing but Charlotte felt quite elated by their discussion. She had to be so careful. She remembered a few weeks ago when she had made soft boiled eggs for tea and when she suggested she cut the toast into soldiers to dip in the eggs as they did when they were children she saw his face freeze. She quickly realised she had said 'soldiers' that was all.

In the afternoon they went for a short stroll, Charlotte wearing a blouse and skirt and Edward wearing a sweater over his warm winceyette shirt. It was true she dreaded the winter. She realised that there was some improvement in him. He was now dressing himself and washing himself too although he needed her help as she carried the basin and hot water jug into his bathroom every time. He wasn't eating enough but he was eating more and was not quite as thin as he had been a year ago when he was discharged from the Army.

Could she manage looking after him on a ship? What would the facilities be? This Dr Drayton in Barbados would be an essential acquaintance. To arrive there with no family one would need friends. What would the people be like there? Would there be any other English people? She realised that from a negative attitude she had had originally, she was starting to think about it seriously. In the days that followed the subject never left her thoughts. Sometimes when she thought Edward was reading her mind drifted away and she was trying to imagine what such a new life would hold. She was startled when

Edward suddenly said "Penny for them?" Charlotte smiled and said "worth a little more darling."

Chapter 6

The Ancestry programme was not able to help her as much as she hoped as she had a lot of missing dates and she decided to 'log off' for a while. The phone rang it was Carrie " I've heard that a pop star from England is staying with your neighbour. Have you seen anyone?" "Well no I haven't exactly been looking" replied Lucy. "Well keep your eyes peeled and ears open and phone me if you see anything" Carrie said in a whisper as though the star might be listening. "Will do. See you later" said Lucy. At first Lucy was annoyed at her work being interrupted by something so trivial. "Hmm" Lucy pondered "it will be a break from my research if I do a bit of scouting" so she opened her door and sauntered down the path between the two houses trying to see or hear anything. She could hear loud music and voices and there seemed to be a lunch party in full flow. There was a high wall between her path and her neighbours drive and there were huge security gates which would only open if the guests knew the code number to press on the little black security box by the gate.

Lucy decided to be adventurous so climbed a tall thin papaya tree which grew in the border next to the joint wall. Her feet kept slipping and she broke a nail trying to get a hold but she thought she had seen a famous face on the patio by the pool and the person kept walking in and out of her sight. The tree swayed slightly with her weight. She climbed just a little higher thinking "get down girl you are too old for these tricks" when a loud voice behind her suddenly said "whilst you are up there could you call for someone to open the gates I've forgotten the code".

She nearly died as she recognised a famous singer and half jumped and half fell out of the tree landing at his feet. He helped her up dusting down the soil from her shoulders but just then someone on the patio saw them and called that they would open the gate. "Oh I am so very sorry" Lucy stumbled over her words but the man laughed and said "Please don't apologise I'm going to eat out on this" as he disappeared down the drive to her neighbours house.

Lucy went back into the cottage and phoned Carrie. They both laughed as Lucy tried to recall exactly what had happened. "Lets lunch at the Golf Club" suggested Carrie, "I'll meet you there at one thirty". Without too much persuasion Lucy agreed. She wandered into her bedroom and changed from baggy shorts and sloppy tee shirt into something a little more respectable. "Ben, I would usually be asking you - how do I look - ok?" she looked up to the ceiling as she spoke. "I know, I look just fine" she nodded. "Red posh tee shirt, tailored white crops so red heeled sandals" she said to herself "mustn't let standards slip" she thought. She added some simple jewellery and a squirt of Tresor perfume and grabbed her bag and car keys after closing the verandah doors and the shutters in the bedrooms. She laughed as she placed her house keys under the upturned blue ceramic plant pot next to the steps outside her door. "No thief would have far to look" she considered as she hurried towards her car.

Valerie Boothman

Chapter 7

Lucy enjoyed lunch with Carrie and a few of her other friends joined them. Maria Mayer-Brown was the wife of Michael Mayer-Brown whose family had been Solicitors on the island since the year dot. She was a very good golfer with a single figure handicap but was very modest about it. Although they lived in a huge house in St. Thomas but there was no edge to either of them and they were good company. Michael was very much involved with horse racing and when Ben was alive he and Lucy were regularly invited as their guests on Gold Cup Day at Garrison Savannah Race Course. Since Ben's death she had declined invitations to large social functions but had accepted invitations to small dinner parties. Most friends understood. Lunch over she walked back to her car with Carrie. "Are you going to re-join the Golf Club?" Carrie quizzed her. "Yes but not just yet" she answered.

As she left the Club Lucy drove along Highway 2 but turned right up the hill rather than turning towards home. Carrie watched Lucy's car turn towards the middle of the island and wondered if she should follow. "No" she thought "I have to let her handle some things on her own". Lucy drove past Farley Hill National Park and continued towards St Nicholas Abbey. When she reached Cherry Tree Hill she pulled off the road and parked the car. She walked slowly through the forest of Mahogany Trees and could just see nearly tucked away from sight the ruins of the Plantation House. Some areas had been boarded up for safety but walking around the house built of coral stone in tje 19th century one could not help but think of what it must have been like in its heyday. The semi circled frontage gave an impression of a ballroom where there must have been wonderful parties. "Oh to have been a fly on the wall" Lucy thought. There was something very very sad about seeing this wonderful old mansion now in such decay. She walked away from the house away from the darkness and up the path through the trees into the sunlight to the wonderful vantage point where you could see the east coast. The view was breathtaking, down through the Morgan Lewis sugar plantations to the Atlantic Ocean. The blue sky was clear with just a wisp of white cloud on the horizon. The huge breakers were pounding the shore creating clouds of foam. Lucy had first seen this view when she and Ben were on their honeymoon. She remembered Ben saying quietly "there is nothing to touch this." Lucy walked slowly back to her car and started the engine. She drove down the hill through the sugar plantation, past St Andrews Church and Belleplaine towards the coast road. It wasn't long before she found herself at Cattlewash.

She parked the car near to where Rob had parked when he was with her. She looked down at her smart sandals and kicked them off into the foot well of the drivers side. She locked the car and walked down the path through the shrubs and bushes to the beach. The breeze was blowing strongly off the sea. She paddled in the waves as she walked along being careful not to splash her crops. She skipped through the water quickly as the waves caught her and splashed her legs. She looked out to sea and wished she could paint the wonderful blue sky with wisps of clouds like stretched cotton wool. Up to the right the hills were covered with verdant vegetation and crops of sugar cane although not to the extent there had been years ago. She looked down at the sand and picked up a handful and held it near to her face. "Hello" she said and smiled. She let the sand fall gently threw her fingers. She had reached the shack where she and Ben used to stop for a drink and Lucy climbed the steps and sat down at one of the rough bench tables where the blue paint was peeling showing more wood than paint. "Yes Mam?" Lucy looked up into the smiling face of a Bajan young woman holding her order pad and pencil and wearing tight but fashionably torn blue jeans and a red tee shirt with 'Liverpool' emblazoned across it. Lucy patted her pockets and realised she had no money with her, only her car keys. "You pay me next time" the woman answered, recognising Lucy's face. "Then just a coke would be wonderful" Lucy said. Lucy looked out to sea watching the Atlantic breakers crash on to the beach as they had done together many times. She walked back to the car slowly, enjoying being there and for once no tears streaming down her cheeks. "That's good" she said to the wind. Ben would understand. She drove home a more direct route but stopped in Speightstown to do some shopping.

As she approached the cottage door she noticed that the blue plant pot was not exactly in the same place as where she had left. She always made a note of the exact position of the pot. Cautiously she entered the cottage. There on the kitchen top was a Mango Cheesecake with a note "You enjoy, Diana". "Ah well" thought Lucy "my old maid is certainly making sure I don't starve but I will have to take half of it up to Carrie and Tom's."

Valerie Boothman

Chapter 8

For several days Lucy did not return to her computer other than to check emails and on a couple of occasions to look up the background of people she had read about in the newspapers. She started to swim every morning as she had when Ben was alive. Then she would sit at her desk and handle the mail and pay a few bills but could not bring herself to start up 'Ancestry' again. She sorted out some accounts about the house in Somerset. It would need a new central heating boiler soon and she would have to attend to that. It didn't seem right to ask the Bennetts to replace it and she would reimburse them but it was tempting. She really ought to contact them. They were good tenants and did an amazing amount of work to the house as though it were their own.

Weeks had passed when one evening before the sun went down Lucy carried the family Bible to the table on the verandah. "This is heavy" she thought, remembering them bringing it back from England. Ben had put it in his cabin baggage and he had made her laugh by calling it 'Holy Moses'. She sauntered into the kitchen and poured herself a Gin and Tonic and returned to the verandah. She was amused that her family had used this wonderful old leather bound book to hold valuable documents. Well valuable in so far as it would be difficult to replace them. Her mother had told her that many families used to have a Family Bible for the same purpose. She recollected searching through the pages looking for her Birth Certificate in her teens when she needed to apply for a Passport. No one else's certificates had interested her then. She was only concerned with finding hers. "Did anyone ever use this Bible for its real purpose" she pondered. The pages were quite thin and edged with gold leaf of which some were torn. The first certificate she found was that of her grandmother Charlotte Spencer born 1890 in Newton Ferrers and her grandfather Edward Richards born 1885 in Plymouth. She also found his death certificate of 1950 when she was only a child. He was aged 61 years. Her grandfather had enlisted in World War One just after he and her grandmother had been married. She knew he had commanded a Trench Mortar Battery and then a mobile Royal Field Artillery battery. He suffered from Neurasthenia, what is now called Post Traumatic Stress Disorder and had never really recovered completely. Lucy found a copy of his discharge paper stating that he was 'unfit for service' and his signature was identifiable across the bottom of the certificate. She saw the words printed in red "Theatre of War" and pondered about the description.

In the Bible Lucy found some receipts of purchases which made no sense to her and she wondered why these small insignificant documents had been saved. The sun was quickly going down so she closed the book and cleared the table before securing the verandah for the night. None of the documents she had found so far had helped her at all in solving the mystery. She loved this time of the evening. The Carib Grackle birds who were unwanted breakfast guests were silent now but in the evening the chorus of the Cicada insects was deafening. "Good Lord" she said aloud "I've been too engrossed in Holy Moses to get a drink". She wandered over to the kitchen area of the cottage and went through the ritual, a good inch of gin, three ice cubes from the small freezer compartment, slice of lime cut from a fresh lime, tonic water from the fridge poured over the ice cubes to within an inch of the rim of the glass. Yet again she watched the line of small bubbles climbing to the top and she shook the glass slightly whilst lifting it to her ear to hear the clink clink of the ice against the glass. " I will tell you something Ben" she whispered "old habits die hard" and she smiled as she went back to the verandah. Lucy started thinking of how many times she spoke to Ben during the day, spoke out loud too. "I wonder if I am going mad?" she said. "Is it normal?" she pondered. She didn't speak to him when anyone else was there so no-one else knew. The strange thing was that although she would talk to him about many things, she never mentioned her research. Was this because he had never shown any interest in the mystery when he was alive? She didn't know. She wondered if there would come a time when she didn't talk to him. She hoped not.

Chapter 9

That night she had a strange dream. She was in England walking in a wooded valley near to where she had once lived. She scrambled over fallen trees scratching herself on brambles. It was Springtime and the wood was full of bluebells. Shafts of sunlight pierced the darkness created by the tall trees. Birds were singing perched high on the branches and she could hear the gurgling sound of water. A small stream meandered through the wood, the water falling over large stones covered in green moss. She followed the path and in the distance she could see her parents sitting on a fence with their backs to her. They were holding hands and laughing. As she approached they turned to look at her. Her mother didn't seem to recognise her but she smiled as you would to a stranger. Then her father put out his hand and helped her to climb the fence. When she woke up she was shivering. She didn't like dreams, they were never happy ones. She looked at her clock it was 6 am so she got out of bed and put on her wrap and went into the kitchen to make a cup of tea.

When it was fully light she put on her swimsuit and walked down the steps, through the garden to the beach. She opened the gate and looked both ways, the beach was deserted. Within seconds she was floating in the clear turquoise water with a feeling of perfect peace washing over her. After a shower Lucy phoned Carrie whilst still wrapped in a large bath towel. "Do you fancy driving over to Crane today to have a look at all the development that's going on there and I'll treat you to lunch?" asked Lucy. "Well that means cancelling a hair appointment" said Carrie "but if it's your treat I can't refuse."

The Crane Hotel on the Atlantic South Coast in the parish of St Philips was a small hotel of about 20 bedrooms in the early 1920's but its position perched on the fossil filled cliff top was, and is, incredible giving magnificent views of the Atlantic Ocean and the coast. It had first opened its doors in 1886 after a civil engineer Donald Simpson bought a villa and turned it into The Crane Hotel. During its long history respective owners had expanded it but the current Canadian owner embarked on a huge expansion of the hotel and site in 1998 creating over 200 suites with ocean views, a Roman swimming pool, tennis courts, restaurants and a shopping village. Wealthy visitors from Europe and America have visited The Crane over many years to experience not only the sun but the freshly purified air which has crossed the ocean from Africa. There was now an elevator down to the beach to replace the precarious steps in the rocks and the narrow bridge.

Lucy pipped her horn as she drove into the drive at Fairmont, Carrie and Tom's house, and Carrie waved as she came down the steps. On their drive over to Crane their conversation was light but Lucy was taken aback when Carrie suddenly said "What is all this research you are doing? Are you writing a book?" Lucy knew that many times when Carrie had popped in to Tamarind uninvited, as friends do, she had been working on her computer and had logged off quickly. Lucy jumped at the idea of her writing a book. She certainly could not quickly think of a better answer. "Oh well yes, I am just dabbling, you know they say there is a book in everyone and I am just playing at it at the moment." "Well I'm your proof reader whenever you need me" said Carrie. Lucy changed the subject as they approached The Crane Hotel. "So what are you in the mood for, Thai, Italian, or fresh seafood?" asked Lucy. "Well my choice would be the L'Azure Restaurant and lets see what's on the menu" Carrie replied.

Their table was in a wonderful position high above the beach looking out over the ocean. Lucy ordered the Blue Swimmer Crab Quesadilla with salad and Carrie chose the same. A bottle of Pinot Grigio went perfectly with their food and the two friends enjoyed the atmosphere and chatted amicably taking a long time over their meal. Lucy pointed to the statues of long-legged cranes scattered around the resort. Carrie said "You know Lucy this place isn't named after the Crane birds? A real crane was positioned on the cliff adjacent to where the hotel is now. The crane lowered and raised cargo from small trading ships which used to sail into the natural harbour." "How long ago was that?" asked Lucy "Not really sure but a long time ago. Not in my life time" laughed Carrie. "It was originally The Marine Villa before they threw money at it but it's been The Crane as long as I can remember" Carrie added. Later they wandered around the shopping village and then made their way over to the car park. On the way home they were strangely quiet yet comfortable in each others company, Lucy being very aware of what a good friend she had in Carrie. She had not been the easiest friend to cope with since Ben's death but Carrie had been patient and always seemed to know when she was needed and when to back off.

Chapter 10

A few weeks passed, then one morning Lucy decided that after breakfast she would resume her search. Lucy carried 'Holy Moses' through to the table on the verandah and sat down. She decided she needed a cup of coffee before she started in earnest so went over to the kitchen and made a cup of instant Nescafe with a little bit of milk and one sweetener laughing as the sweetener made a plop sound as it dropped into the coffee. With no more excuses Lucy sat down and started turning each page carefully so as not to miss anything. She had a note book and wrote down anything she saw which she thought was of special interest. It was a laborious task trying to make sure she missed nothing. Some of the small receipts fascinated her.

There were companies who she had never heard of and some were so old they were illegible. She wondered why at one time these little bits of paper had been important. Although she was desperate to study the documents more closely her eyes were aching, she needed a break and her coffee had gone cold. She walked over to the kitchen and threw away the cold coffee and made a fresh cup. She went over to her desk and opened a drawer taking out a silver handled magnifying glass. She needed more than contact lenses and reading glasses to study these documents.

Lucy sat at the table looking out to sea through the branches of the huge mahogany tree. She sipped her coffee. The birds were quiet. The monkeys who sometimes jumped around were nowhere to be seen. She could hear the gentle sound of small waves lapping the beach. She was aware of a quietness, a stillness, and serenity. "Why?" she wondered, "was she on the brink of something? Why should she think that?" She returned to the Bible ready to continue.

She turned several pages where she found nothing of interest then she came across a small piece of paper tucked nearly into the spine of the book. It had yellowed and was very thin. It bore printing and some hand writing. Lucy ironed out the creases with the palms of her hand and tried to read the printed name on the top of the document. It read 'Goodrich & Waters' and below in smaller print it read ' Solicitors, Civil Litigation, 16 Water Street, Bridgetown, Barbados. Est. 1904.' She could feel goose pimples on her arms, her back stiffened and she gazed at this small document in amazement. Why should a document from a Solicitors in Bridgetown, Barbados be placed in her family Bible? All the other documents were either Birth, Marriage and Death Certificates or were connected to England.

The ink of the hand writing had faded. She looked very closely at the wording. She tried to decipher the name of the client, it was written in long hand and she thought it might say Mr & Mrs Richards but it was very faint. She could just identify 'In receipt of £100 for our attention and service.' A signature had been scrawled beneath. It looked as though the surname was 'Waters' but the first name was illegible. At the foot of the receipt there was a date 'February 28th 1920'. She looked in the telephone directory but could not find Goodrich & Waters. The name sounded familiar to her but the Solicitors she and Ben had used were called Meyer-Brown & Hanschell because they knew them through the Golf Club. Lucy decided to phone Maria Meyer-Brown to see if she could find out anything from her. Maria asked "What's this? Are we losing your business?" when Lucy asked about the names of other Solicitors. Lucy assured her that was not the case and they both laughed but Lucy was not prepared to explain further. "I'll get Mike to phone you when he gets in" said Maria. Lucy decided to see what more she could find in the Bible and this time she was even more careful scrutinising every small piece of paper. Her head was spinning and as Carrie and Tom were coming for supper that evening she closed 'Holy Moses' and carried him through to her bedroom placing him on a book shelf. "Is this receipt important?" she asked herself.

Valerie Boothman

Chapter 11

She locked the house and walked along the beach to the fish market, it was a good walk, nearly a mile but she enjoyed the exercise. "Enough Tuna for three" she told Barnaby. As usual he gave her enough for six but she always enjoyed left over Tuna with a salad so there was no problem. Whilst she was waiting for the fish to be prepared she looked across the road to the rum shop. The music was loud and a group of boys were helping a Coca Cola wagon to unload his delivery. The wooden crates of Coke and Fanta Orange were piled high on a sack truck and the handler was struggling to drag it over the kerb. They were singing, dancing and laughing, wearing brightly coloured tee shirts and Bata flip-flops on their feet. She knew one of them and he waved to her. "There you go lady" said Barnaby so she paid him and wandered back along the beach. Boys were playing cricket with a piece of wood for a bat and an old tennis ball. She remembered when she and Ben first came to Barbados it was commonplace to see 'would be' future West Indian cricketers playing cricket along the coast dodging the waves and shouting if they had to go into the sea to retrieve the ball. She assumed technology had spoilt all that. Play Stations and computers were more exciting than a game on the beach. The influence from America of Basketball as seen on their TV's also played its part. "It's a shame" Lucy thought.

When she walked into Tamarind Lucy noticed there was a message light on her 'phone so she picked it up. "Hi Lucy. What's this checking up on my competitors?" it was Mike's voice. "Well Goodrich & Waters are now Bailey,

Goodrich & Waters they took on a new partner many years ago but that's why you didn't find them in the directory Lucy. Take care hope to see you soon" Mike had rung off. Lucy checked the Telephone Directory for the number then picked up the phone and dialled. She asked if she could make an appointment to see one of the senior partners. She suggested Mr Waters Senior and felt rather stupid when she was told he had retired some years ago. "Shall I see if Mr James Waters could see you?" suggested the receptionist and Lucy agreed. The appointment was made for the following Wednesday so Lucy started preparing that night's supper. She would keep it simple. She marinated the tuna in rum, herbs and seasoning the way her maid had taught her. She would leave the salad and cou cou (yellow cornmeal with okras) for later. Lucy skipped lunch and went for a swim draping a large beach towel round her shoulders. Water skiers were speeding through the water but they kept a safe distance from the beach. Walking back from the beach through the garden she realised she was looking forward to entertaining the Porters tonight. Tom and Carrie were always good company. Lucy washed the sand from her feet using water from the garden tap by her steps and managed to dry them before entering the cottage. She sat on the verandah with her towel wrapped round her, brushing her hair slowly in long strokes until it had nearly dried. She lent back in her chair with eyes closed and wondered what lay ahead for her. She knew she was getting close to something, but what?

The evening was a great success. Low key and for the first time in a while Lucy felt happy. The three friends sat on the verandah listening to Barbers Adagio for Strings just chatting in the easy way only old friends can. The haunting melody was so beautiful that conversation stopped and they just listened to the music, sipping wine and occasionally glancing at each other and smiling. At times such as these the cicadas seemed to fall quiet as though they knew they should not compete. As the music ended Tom stood up and gathered the empty glasses. Carrie helped Lucy to clear the table and then it was a joint effort closing up the shutters and doors. Lucy waved her away as Carrie offered to stack the dishes in the machine. They thanked her warmly for a lovely evening and she watched as they walked through the darkness, up the path to their car.

Chapter 12

Wednesday arrived. Lucy knew it may be difficult to park at the Solicitors as their offices were in an old part of Bridgetown where the streets are narrow. She parked near the top of Broad Street where the bronze statue of Admiral Lord Nelson stood, erected in 1813 predating the one in Trafalgar Square in London by thirty years. The Barbadians had appreciated Nelsons efforts fighting the French at a time when they controlled some of the other islands in the Caribbean. Nelson visited Barbados in 1805. The French and the British were often battling for ownership and several islands changed hands frequently. Barbados however remained under British rule until independence in 1966. Trafalgar Square was renamed National Heroes Square in 1999 but the area is often referred to by many as Trafalgar.

Lucy walked quickly although she knew she was not late, just nervous. The receptionist was pleasant and suggested Lucy sat in the waiting room. On the stark white walls were brown wooden framed certificates showing the partner's qualifications. Lucy straightened her skirt and buttoned up the bottom button. She considered how she should put her questions to Mr Waters, it was vital to the success of her visit. A gentleman smartly dressed in grey trousers and white short sleeved shirt, wearing a grey and navy tie loosely knotted at his neck, came down the stairs and put forward his hand saying "Mrs Harrison, I'm James Waters, pleased to meet you". He motioned that she should follow him upstairs and along a short corridor into his office. The office had a nice feel to it. One wall was filled with book cases containing old leather backed books, some a deep red colour and others black and brown with gold lettering on their spine. Wooden panelling filled the other walls and there were photographs of family members on one wall. There was a high window through which sunlight lit the room. She wondered if the receipt in her possession had been written in this very office. "So what can I do for you Mrs Harrison?" It took Lucy several seconds to compose herself before she started to explain her visit.

She slowly opened the file she had been carrying. She showed James Waters the receipt she had found in the family Bible. He smiled and said "It is not unusual for families to keep documents for safe keeping this way." He smoothed out the document with the tips of his fingers whilst studying it very closely. He frowned then looked up. " How can I help you Mrs Harrison?" he asked. She explained that she had always been aware of an uneasy silence whenever Barbados was mentioned in her family. She was trying to find some reason why her parents would never agree to come to Barbados. I cannot trace any record of her birth in England. Now she had found a receipt from a Solicitors office in Barbados dated the same year that her mother had been born. She asked Mr Waters to look closely at the name of the client. She asked if it were possible that the name was Richards, the surname of her grandparents?

"I really could not say, what are you hoping to achieve Mrs Harrison, this is all very tenuous?" said James Waters. Lucy replied "I am trying to find out where my mother was born.. Was she born in Barbados? If so why has it been a secret? If she was born in England why is there no trace of a birth record there? I have been checking the records on the Internet and can find none." James Waters looked very concerned. "Mrs Harrison, with the greatest respect you are an amateur at tracing your family's records it may be worthwhile employing a professional to search for the record of your mothers birth in England". Lucy felt that she was failing to express her need for help "Mr Waters do you have records going back to 1920 which may explain this receipt which is undoubtedly for work carried out by your company?" pleaded Lucy. "This receipt may have no connection with your family. I cannot explain why it was in their possession but we have to exercise complete discretion and privacy towards our clients" James Waters explained. Lucy looked downcast. "Would you still have the records?" asked Lucy very quietly. "Any documentation in our care which has not been collected by those to whom it refers, is destroyed after a period of time" he said. "What is that period of time" asked Lucy, "usually fifty years sometimes we keep them longer" answered James Waters.

"Mrs Harrison do not hold out any hope. If we were able to trace documentation for the work relating to this receipt and our client bore no connection to yourself, we are duty bound by solemn oath not to pass it to another person". Lucy nodded "I understand Mr Waters" she said. Lucy realised that the appointment had come to an end. "Mr Waters" said Lucy "my husband died within the last year. My parents are dead and my son lives in Australia. It is paramount to me to trace my mother's birth. I cannot just accept that nothing can be done when I am convinced that this receipt is the key to my peace of mind. I will employ experts in England to look for any record of my mothers birth there and I will also now study records in Barbados.

I do not wish to offend you but could I ask that you consult your partners and explain my situation and perhaps this noble company may at the very least examine their records of February 1920".

Lucy stood up holding her head high. James Waters smiled at her description of his company. She withdrew her chequebook from her handbag. "There will be no charge Mrs Harrison. Let me see what I can do but I make no promises" he said as he shook her outstretched hand. She had mixed emotions as she drove back to Tamarind from Bridgetown. She had planned to do a bit of shopping in Da Costa whilst in the capital but she was in no mood.

Chapter 13
1919

Two days before Edward's parents were due to arrive Charlotte knew a decision had to be made. The easiest decision was to decline, no one would blame her. What if then Edward fell ill in the winter, how would she feel. She suddenly realised that she had made the decision, they would go. How and when should she discuss the subject with Edward.

After lunch she suggested they took a walk. As always Edward agreed. "Another lovely day Edward" she said as they strolled along the flat part of the lane which then slowly rose up the hill. He nodded "if only the weather was always like this" he said as he smiled at her and patted her arm which was linked in his. When they walked up the hilly part they didn't speak so that Edward could manage his breathing better. "Lets sit down here" Charlotte said as they reached an old bench. They sat looking down at the creek and the river and counted the boats bobbing about in the harbour. It was time to raise the matter she thought. "Edward there is a possibility that you and I could spend next winter in the Caribbean" she said. Edward looked at her "so that is what Papa wanted to speak to you about last week" he said angrily. She waited for several minutes before continuing "Edward your Papa only wants what is best for you."

Edward made a peculiar gruff noise which sounded as though he doubted that statement. He said "I know now that I am ill and lame he can't bear to see me, I am not going to be the son and heir he was expecting me to be" he said quietly. "Darling that really is unfair, you must not take your own disappointments out on your father." Edward looked at her for a long time. "Oh dear Charlotte, I promised you the world and what have I given you?" Charlotte said "my dear you promised me your love and if I still have that then I am happy."

They sat on the seat for quite a long time and then Edward said "We aren't going Charlotte" he frowned. "I would be sea sick and I don't want changes". She smiled. "Papa told me that we have to make a decision quickly but I think this is too soon for us both. We need more time." They rose from the seat and slowly walked down the hill to the little cottage which nestled in the hill side. Signs of the honeysuckle which would cover the porch entrance were clearly visible. The hollyhocks and delphiniums would be reaching for the sky in the summer. They would spend lazy days listening to the sounds of the lawn mowers from neighbours gardens and smelling the cut grass. The small white yachts would be racing in the harbour. Edward decided they definitely would not be going to Barbados.

The day dawned for the visit of Edward's parents to Newton Ferrers. When Adam and Emily Richards arrived at the cottage they were pleased to see that Edward looked better than on their last visit. It was unfortunate that he had a severe bout of coughing and Charlotte had to administer the cough medicine. They spoke of pleasantries and then Adam asked Charlotte would she like to take a short walk with him down the lane. "No Papa" said Edward "whatever you wish to discuss you do in my presence." Adam was taken aback, his son had never been so rude to him in his life. "I beg your pardon

Sir" Adam said "I will not be spoken to in that fashion." Emily was embarrassed and wrung her hands together and said "I will make a cup of tea" and disappeared into the kitchen. After a few more angry words Charlotte put her hands up and said "enough, enough, this can be discussed civilly I beg you."

When no one had spoken for several minutes Charlotte said "Papa, Edward and I have discussed your kind offer for us to winter in Barbados. It would be a huge undertaking and cannot be decided in such a short space of time." Edward interrupted her and said "We are not going." Charlotte continued "we would appreciate your allowing us a little while longer before we give you our decision." "We are not going the decision has been made" said Edward. Emily's sobs could be heard from the kitchen, she had been listening to their conversation.

Charlotte was standing behind Edward facing his father so Edward could not see her face. She smiled at Adam Richards who was looking very angry and upset and was shaking his head. "As you can see Papa it is probable that we will not accept your generous offer and will stay in England this winter but please give us another seven days before we say definitely 'no'." As Charlotte said this she managed to wink at Adam Richards praying that he would not re-act to her actions. A tearful Emily emerged from the kitchen with a tray of tea. The tea was drunk with little conversation and it was as well that it was soon time for the older Richards to depart. The meeting had tired Edward and he had disappeared into his room to lie down. Adam looked at Charlotte and said "ladies like you are made in heaven" and quickly took his wife's arm and walked out of the door.

Charlotte's thoughts were in turmoil. She wasn't even sure herself that they should go to Barbados let alone convince Edward but she knew that last winter she had nearly lost Edward when he caught pneumonia. She believed that the good work building up his strength in the summer could be undone next winter. In her heart of hearts she knew she needed all her skills and guile to persuade him. After tea she took down a box from a high shelf where she stored board games. That evening they sat across from each other doing a jigsaw puzzle. Edward enjoyed evenings such as this until he tired. She carefully placed all the pieces the right side up and said "lets look for the corner pieces first Edward and then the sides and work inwards, shall we?" Edward nodded. They found the four corner pieces and then Edward said "let me have a look at the lid of the box Charlotte, let me see the picture so we know our next steps." Charlotte passed him the lid, the picture showed a beach scene on a tropical island. Edward stood up "not very subtle" he said angrily and knocked over the table. He limped towards his room and slammed the door.

Charlotte thought he was right, it hadn't been very subtle but she was angry with him for his childish reaction. Usually she would have followed him into his room and begged forgiveness and helped him to prepare for bed but not this time. She decided the time had come for the nurse to show some mettle. She picked up all the pieces of the jigsaw and placed them in the box and put the box back on the shelf. She heard him moving around but was determined not to weaken. She sat reading by the fire finding it very difficult to actually take in the words before her. She made herself a cup of cocoa to help her sleep and returned to her chair. When all was quiet in Edwards room she crept over to his door and lifted the latch. The eider-down had fallen on to the floor so she picked it up and spread it out over him. She could see he was asleep but he was still wearing the shirt he had worn during the day. She tiptoed out of his room carefully dropped the latch and went upstairs to her bedroom. Edward opened one eye and then closed it quickly and gave a huge sigh.

Chapter 14

Lucy parked the car and touched the sticky sweet smelling frangipani flowers as she walked down the path to her door. The key was under the blue ceramic plant pot. She opened up the wide verandah doors and the sun flooded the house. The smart navy suit went back into the wardrobe and she stepped into the shower. She lifted her face to the tumbling water and enjoyed the sensation. She felt she was cleansing herself from a stuffy Solicitors office. The consultation had not gone according to plan. She felt frustrated but why, had she expected more? All she had found was a small receipt from a Solicitors in Bridgetown, Barbados. She sensed that in spite of James Waters dismissal of her request for him to investigate their archives, he seemed to know something. One thing she would do is get a professional to search for records of her mothers birth in England.

Lucy sent an email to her Solicitor in England. She knew his daughter, a lady called Jenny Crossman was a professional Genealogist. She was a very competent researcher of family history and Lucy could trust her to leave no stone unturned. She gave her as many details as she would need and said there was no real urgency but sooner rather than later would be appreciated. About a week later she received a report from Jenny advising her that her search had been in vain. In many ways this did not surprise Lucy but at least she had a copy of Jenny's report which showed her credentials and proved that Lucy had followed James Waters advice.

Lucy decided to visit the Barbados Department of

National Archives where Birth, Marriages and Death records were held. She knew the office was in Black Rock in St Michael, just around the corner from the University. It had been two weeks since her meeting with James Waters and she had heard nothing. Lucy asked for assistance and then laboriously looked for records of the birth of a Susan Louise Richards born in February 1920. She found nothing. For some reason, grasping at straws, she decided to look for a child under her grandmothers maiden name of Spencer but found no entry under that name. She was beginning to lose hope. The clerk was very kind and looked sadly at Lucy as she handed back the microfilms. Lucy felt very frustrated as she left the office and drove home. "I am going to find you Susan Louise Barnes, nee Susan Louise Richards, I am going to find you Mum" she said out loud.

It had started to go dark and she knew they were in for a tropical storm. She hated driving in really heavy rain and the journey home was usually forty minutes if the traffic wasn't too bad. She drove past Sandy Lane Hotel where all the celebrities stayed and remembered how a very long time ago she and Ben and some friends had once enjoyed Sunday Lunch there and had a dip in the pool but now it was only for the very rich and famous. As she passed St Alban's Church it was raining stair rods but she knew she was getting close to home so relaxed. She drove into the small drive behind Tamarind and quickly parked the car. She ran as fast as she could to her door and fumbled with the keys in her wet hands as the rain was streaming down her face. It was such a good feeling to get into the house and leave her shoes by the door. Her clothes were saturated so she stripped off in her bedroom and stepped into the shower. She lifted her face to the hot water exclaiming with joy at the sensation as the gushing water spilled over her. Wrapped in a white towelling robe she made a cup of coffee. Lucy walked over to the verandah and opened one door so that she could sit and watch the rain splashing off the large solid branches of the mahogany trees. The sad red blossoms of the Hibiscus in the garden below were taking a battering. She always thought it quite marvellous how they recovered so quickly. She held her coffee mug in both hands and as she sipped the coffee thought about what actual facts she had to go on. Not many. She decided to place them in order of merit or order of importance. Strangely enough, number one was the knowledge that she had been unable to bring her mother to Barbados and that throughout her life the island had been a subject not to be mentioned. Number two was the fact that there was no record of her mothers birth in England. Number three, well that had to be the receipt she had found. There really wasn't an order of merit they were all equal but she had to admit she didn't have very much. Looking for the Births in February 1920 by surname had found nothing.

That evening Rob phoned from Australia to ask how she was. Her head was full of births, marriages and deaths and she found it difficult to concentrate. Rob asked if she was alright so she tried her best to sound normal. "Have you rejoined Westmoreland" asked Rob. "No not yet I've been too busy to play golf but I will do soon" Lucy said. "Too busy, doing what?" Rob asked with an incredulous edge to his voice. "Oh please don't worry I am fine, honestly, I am thinking next year I may come for a visit" she thought that would put his mind at rest. "Fantastic old girl, we would all love to see you, stay as long as you want" Rob assured her.   Visiting Australia was the last thing on her mind at the moment but she knew they worried about her.

Chapter 15
1919

Charlotte awoke to some strange noises down stairs. She grabbed her wrap and hurried down. Edward was stumbling around in the kitchen in his dressing gown making tea. Most of his actions were with his right hand as he needed to hold his stick in his left hand to stop him from falling over.

"Can I help?" asked Charlotte. "You may take the tray" said Edward. "Lets go back to your room and I will get in bed with you and we will drink our tea there" suggested Charlotte. Edward looked at Charlotte with the most wonderful expression on his face and said "We will."

Charlotte puffed up the pillows so they could both sit up straight holding their tea cups in their hands, it was easier without saucers. They sipped the hot tea but said nothing. Then Edward took Charlotte's empty cup from her and placed it on the tray. He turned to her and took her in his arms and held her close for several minutes. Then he said "well please help me to get washed and dressed and then if it is fine we can walk up to the seat on the hill, we have many plans to make . . . for Barbados." Charlotte kissed him and arose from the bed.

Charlotte sent a message to her father in law telling him of their decision to winter in the Caribbean and suggesting he went ahead with the plans. She told him she would be in Plymouth the following Wednesday to visit the Library as she needed to borrow books about the climate and the kind of clothes to wear. She suggested calling on them around 2 o clock and said she hoped Mama had not taken it too badly and that she would come to terms with their decision.

Charlotte was amazed how quickly Edward started looking forward to going. He kept saying "it will be warm, won't it Charlotte?" Charlotte said "yes I believe sometimes too warm and we will have to wear different clothes to these" as she held up her warm skirt. "We must look forward to it as an adventure Edward, it isn't forever, just over the winter, and you know how you hate the cold." Edward said "I am much better now aren't I Charlotte, not so many bad dreams?" Charlotte looked at him and smiled "we have to be patient, they will go sometime." She prayed she was right.

So in late August 1919 the docks in Southampton were busy. The Royal Mail Packet Steamer was nearly ready to leave. Charlotte's parents and Edward's parents had settled Charlotte and Edward on board and had returned to the quay. They were standing together waving as the ship pulled away from the docks. Emily was in a terrible mess with tears streaming down her cheeks and she was comforted by Margaret Spencer Charlotte's mother who was trying to hold back the tears. Emily wondered where Charlotte had found the strength to take this voyage with a sick husband and no family nor friends to support her. Charlotte left Edward in their cabin to go on deck and wave to their family as the Steamer gently moved away. Moved away from everything dear to her. She did not wait long on deck and soon returned to Edward who she knew would be worried without her. She wondered what the future held for them both.

Chapter 16

Lucy swept the floor of the verandah. Apart from the puddles there was no sign of the tropical storm of the previous evening and everywhere was green and fresh. She had agreed to visit an old friend, Rachael Davidson, for coffee who had an apartment at the marina in Port St Charles. This would be a fifteen minute drive north. On the way there she intended to stop and buy fruit from the ladies whose fruit stalls were on the side of the road in Speightstown. She liked to support them and their fruit was always fresh. They wore brightly coloured dresses and turbans round their heads and were always cheerful and friendly.

She knew she wanted a few oranges and a couple of papayas, that was what she liked to eat for breakfast. She pulled off the road just north of the town centre and chatted whilst she selected the fruit. They always tried to sell her twice as much as she wanted. As she drove into Port St Charles the Security Guard waved her on as he knew she was a regular visitor. She could see Rachael waving from her balcony as she parked the car. She had coffee with her old friend and Rachael said it was good to see her getting around and managing a life without Ben.

She had been a widow for ten years herself so they swapped stories of how friends tried to help them, many quite amusing stories and Lucy said "it's good to laugh". Rachael nodded and as she looked up they exchanged glances knowing they had much in common. Lucy explained that she couldn't stay for lunch as she had many things to do but they agreed to meet again soon. She decided to tell Rachael that she had been trying to trace the possible birth of an ancestor in Barbados but had had no luck tracing the surname. It was typical of Rachael that she didn't press her further but she said "Why don't you tell the assistants at the Archives Records Office exactly what you are looking for and give them whatever information you do have. I have found them to be very skilled, trust them". "I will" said Lucy "I will, good idea".

As Lucy drove away from Port St Charles she decided the next stop in her quest was to look at Church Parish Records. That way she could look by date and see if any entry could relate to her family. So, rather than turn into Tamarind she drove past the turning and continued towards Bridgetown. As she approached St Michael she took the road towards Black Rock. The archives were housed in the old Leper Hospital, Old Lazaretto, where she had been the previous day. Old Lazaretto had been used for the safe keeping of old documents since 1964. Lucy parked the car and this time she explained what she was looking for to an assistant. The girl looked at Lucy and then said to follow her to her desk. "I'm Joanna, Mrs Harrison" she said. "Oh please call me |Lucy" Lucy replied.

Joanna entered a search engine well known for tracing family history. She looked through several countries and clicked on "Caribbean Births Marriages and Deaths'. She looked up and smiled at Lucy. She then found a page headed Caribbean Births and Baptisms 1590 - 1928. The next stage was to fill in some details. "First name?" Joanna asked. "Susan" said Lucy. "Surname?" Lucy said "Richards" "Date of birth?" Lucy said "10th February 1920" Joanna pressed 'enter' and the page read 'No Records'. When Joanna saw the expression on Lucy's face she quickly said "Whoah we aren't beaten yet. Did she have another first name?" "Yes, Louise" said Lucy. So this time Joanna entered Louise as the first name. There were no results. Then Joanna suggested they put in all the information again but left out the surname. They were still unsuccessful. Joanna said "Here we go again" entering the first name as Louise but no surname. The page changed and Lucy bent over Joanna's shoulder to try to see the screen. Joanna moved away and let Lucy sit down. There was a record of a baptism.

The record read: Baptised 28th February, Born 10th February, Childs name - Louise, Parents name - Louise Balfour, (there was no fathers name) Abode of parent - Fairfields, Profession - Scholar, Ceremony performed by - Rev. Charles Courtney. Beneath these details it read Baptism solemnised in the Parish of the Church of St John in the Island of Barbados in the year 1920. Joanna looked at Lucy " Do you think this could be what you are looking for or shall we continue our search?" Lucy sat quietly for several seconds. This was really just the record of a girl named Louise baptised in St Johns Church, with the same birth date as her mother, that was all. However Lucy then said "this may be the one, is it possible to get a copy of this record? I'll look no further for the moment." Joanna nodded and Lucy followed her to another department where a copy was produced.

Lucy said goodbye and walked towards her car shaking her head in disbelief. She realised that she must not jump to conclusions. Firstly there must have been other babies born on 10th February 1920 in Barbados, if this is where her mother was born. If this record of baptism did relate to her mother then why was the baby's name listed as

Louise and not Susan Louise. Why was the mother not shown as Charlotte Richards? Who was Louise Balfour? Why no fathers name? Driving home she realised that there was little hope that this document in her file, beside her on the passenger seat, had any connection with her family. Before she started looking again she would visit James Waters the Solicitor. He knew something and he could at the very least tell her if this document had any credibility in her search. When she arrived home she made a phone call to Bailey Goodrich & Waters and arranged to see James Waters the following Friday.

Chapter 17

On Friday, out came the navy suit again, then she changed her mind, she wasn't trying to impress anyone so crops and a smart white blouse seemed fine. Her fingers touched the gold chain round her neck which Ben had given her for their Ruby Wedding, "if you only knew" she said to him quietly.

James Waters greeted her warmly "Please sit down Lucy, and would you like some tea?" he asked. "Typical of Barbados" she thought "first meeting I am Mrs Harrison but second meeting I am Lucy!" One of the girls brought a tray of tea and poured a cup for them both. James smiled at Lucy and said "Well?" Lucy spread out in front of him the report from the Genealogist in England which proved she had kept her promise. No record of her mother's birth in England. She then showed him the birth record for a girl named Louise born 10th February 1920 to a Louise Balfour with no fathers name. Lucy said "Mr Waters I don't really know why I am so certain but I think my mother was born in Barbados. However I can find no trace of her birth here under my grandparents surname. I have found this record of a baby born 10th February 1920 and baptised in St John's church. She was baptised Louise. Her mother was named Louise Balfour and as you can see there is no fathers name". Lucy looked up and stared at James Waters. She continued " Is this a wild goose chase or am I on the right tracks, if so Mr Waters, then who is Louise Balfour? The birth was registered on the 28th February 1920, the very same date of the receipt in my family Bible."

James Waters examined the documents carefully. "Oh dear" he said shaking his head, "this is unbelievably complicated". "I really don't know where we go from here" he added. "So there is somewhere to go, your partners do know something which you are holding back from me, what records, what documentation do you have?" Lucy pleaded with him.

James Waters finished his tea and stood up confirming to Lucy that he was going to say no more. Lucy stayed seated. She was not going to be dismissed again. James sat down. "These matters concern not my generation, not even my fathers generation but my grandfather's generation" he said. Lucy stared at him. "These matters concern me, here and now" she added. James stretched across the table and took her hands in his. "Lucy you must leave this with me, I promise you that I will do all in my power to help you. I have to speak to stubborn old men who live in the past. They have good values and scruples and the reputation of this firm of Solicitors may be at stake. I don't wish to ruin that but sometimes difficult decisions have to be made. I will be in contact with you very soon". Lucy said "Is this document worthless or do I keep it?" James looked her straight in the eye and said "keep it". That spoke volumes to Lucy. She rose, shook hands with him and could see from his expression that he was troubled.

Driving back to Tamarind Lucy felt very confused. She couldn't concentrate on anything but this mystery. Carrie and Tom had told her they were worried that she was spending too much time on the book she was supposed to be writing. She didn't like telling them lies all the time and she also felt that Carrie did not believe her but was

Valerie Boothman

too good a friend to pry. Lucy parked her car at Holetown and walked over to the post office to purchase stamps. She walked through a gap in the buildings to the beach. The Sports Bar was busy with tourists but she stopped and ordered an orange juice with ice. There were several stalls selling brightly coloured Batik beach wraps and trade seemed good. Loud music was playing. She could hear a conversation at a table near to her where some tourists were saying that they were on a cruise ship and had just caught a taxi up the West Coast from Bridgetown where they had docked. Lucy laughed to herself thinking that the man had been happy to find a Sports Bar where he could watch a televised football match from England but the wife looked as though in the small time they would have on the island, she would rather have seen more of Barbados.

Should she call on Carrie on the way home? It was always difficult to lie immediately after she had done something she could not reveal, like going to the Solicitors, so she drove home. She remembered that as it was Friday Carrie would be playing golf. Lucy showered and put on a lilac coloured tee shirt and purple shorts. She looked in the long mirror "lady in lavender" she said. Her friends teased her because she often wore different shades of purple, she liked the colour. She messed about tidying the garden, reading and writing birthday cards. She quite enjoyed days messing about doing all sorts of little jobs but her mind was on other things. When she arrived home there was a message on the answering machine from Carry saying that the Mosses who were old friends wanted Lucy to come to supper with Carrie and Tom some time soon. She appreciated that old friends were keeping in touch and wanted their friendship to continue even though Ben was no longer around.

Lucy found the next few days very difficult, she did not want to be out of the house if James Waters called. Whenever she did leave the house, the first thing she would do was to check for telephone messages. Then one morning when she was in the shower the 'phone rang. Wrapped in a towel with water dripping everywhere she answered the telephone. She heard James Waters voice say "Lucy can you come to my office tomorrow at about 10am?" She could hardly speak although she knew there was no guarantce that the news would be good. She was sure she would now learn more. "I will be there" she answered quietly.

Chapter 18

Lucy sat in his waiting room, she had been early but it was now 10.10 am and if she had ever bitten her nails she was convinced she would be biting them now. She stared at the white walls and kept breathing deeply trying to settle her nerves. His Secretary apologised that Mr Waters was with another client but was aware that she was waiting and would be with her as soon as possible. At last she heard his steps on the stairs and he apologised profusely for keeping her waiting. She followed him. James Waters sat down at his desk and motioned for Lucy to sit across from him.

She looked at the peeling leather on the surface of his desk and wondered how old it was. "Lucy" said James Waters staring at her kindly. "There is more research you must carry out yourself, I am not able to repeat gossip from years ago. My company deal with facts and at this moment the best I can do is to point you in the right direction". Lucy looked down at her hands in dismay and then looked up to meet James Waters gaze. She looked towards the window but her eyes did not see the bright blue sky. She looked back at his face. "You know something, you know something that I should know" she said. James Waters took her hands in his across the desk "you need to investigate Louise Balfour and her family. From the record you now have you know quite a lot about her. Visit the archives of The Barbados Advocate newspaper, then called The Advocate" he said. Study the birth certificate and when you have more information come back to me." James Waters waited for several minutes, "look at the date on the birth certificate of the baby Louise" he said. "Think this out for yourself". "Do they still have copies of so long ago?" asked Lucy. "Well The Advocate was established in 1895 and I understand they have microfilm of copies from the early 1900's" he said. "What if I find nothing?" asked Lucy. James went very quiet and then said "Look at copies for 1919 and 1920 and come back to see me when you have searched, we have more to discuss but this search must be carried out by you". Lucy thanked him and walked out of his offices wondering what she had thanked him for.

She walked towards where her car was parked with her head spinning and drove to the Barbados Advocate Newspaper Archive offices. The receptionist was very helpful and re-directed her to the correct office. When she arrived she wasn't sure what to do but she asked for the microfilm copy of the newspaper for 1919. The assistant showed her how to load and work the microfilm recorder. She just did not know what she was looking for. Lucy started reading the newspaper from the beginning of the year. She became engrossed in reports of black Bajans emigrating to Panama in their thousands in the first decade of the twentieth century to help dig the Panama Canal. It was stated that many sent money back to Barbados to their families and in some cases money for their wives to travel to Panama and join them. About half of the 19,000 who emigrated had returned to Barbados with their savings intact. In another article it mentioned the abolition of slavery in 1834 which was followed by a four year apprenticeship period where free men continued to work a 45 hour week without pay in exchange for living in tiny huts provided by the plantation owners. She realised just how ignorant she was about this island. "I am just going to have to concentrate better and not be

Valerie Boothman

diverted by interesting stories" she told herself. She had reached May 1919 way but she had developed a head ache staring at the small print and trying not to miss anything which may relate to her family. She walked over to the water dispenser and carried a plastic cup back to where she was sitting and slowly sipped the cold water. She continued her search and tried very hard not to stray from the purpose of her visit. Lucy had just decided that she could look no more that day, she would stop when she reached the end of the month and come back another day. She read that a huge May Day Ball had been held on the Saturday May 3rd 1919, the nearest Saturday to May 1st. It had been held at The Marine Hotel in Hastings, Barbados. She had heard that The Marine was once a huge hotel but now is the site of the Pommarine Hotel, a teaching hotel attached to Barbados Community College.

From the report it had obviously been a very glamorous evening with an orchestra playing and extravagant catering. She read that the enjoyment of the evening was marred by the event which took place towards the end of the evening when the police had been called. She thought that was probably not unusual. She scanned the newspaper for anything that might possibly relate to her but could find nothing. She read anything and everything and felt that she really was looking for a needle in a haystack. There was another mention of the party at The Marine. This time it said that the Police had taken a youth into custody connected with the event which had taken place at The Marine Hotel on 3rd May 1919 and he had been charged with assault and rape. "Oh dear how awful" Lucy said to herself and then continued looking through the papers. After a few minutes she found a report which told her that a youth of 16 years would attend the Juvenile

Justice Section of The Magistrates Court charged with rape of a 14 year old girl. Lucy flinched. It wasn't easy to continue looking for something when she didn't know what she was looking for and her mind kept going back to the rape case even though she never dreamt it should concern her personally. After turning several pages Lucy came across a name she recognised, Balfour. The report said that Daniel Balfour of Fairfields Plantation St Philip had been charged with being drunk and disorderly and threatening Mr David Keppel at Mr Keppel's estate in a neighbouring parish. The Magistrate had shown leniency due to recent events and understood Mr Balfour's anger. However he must allow the Courts to exercise justice and punishment if the accused is found guilty and not take it upon himself to bring revenge. Daniel Balfour was bound over to keep the peace and warned that a repeat of such behaviour would result in sever punishment. Lucy went back to the report of the Police being called to The Marine Hotel on May 1st 1919. She kept saying to herself "no, no, I am reading something into this which isn't there." She sat with her elbows on the table holding her chin in her hands staring at the screen. She thought "this is a nightmare, it can't be, it can't be."

Lucy then started counting back the facts. May 3rd 1919 an event at The Marine Hotel the Police were called. Then it was reported that a youth was taken into custody charged with rape. Then Daniel Balfour of Fairfields St Philip was charged with being drunk and using threatening behaviour towards a David Kepple and the Magistrate was lenient with him because of recent events. Why would Daniel Balfour be so angry and why would the Magistrate be lenient unless he sympathised with him. Who was David Kepple? Was Daniel Balfour related to

Louise Balfour? Fairfields was the place given as her abode on the birth record. Had Louise Balfour been raped?

The clerk approached her and advised her that the office was closing for the day. Lucy could not believe that she had been there all day, it was Friday and their offices would not open until Monday morning. Should she phone James Waters? Should she tell him what she had discovered? No, she decided she would return to The Advocate archive offices on Monday morning and see what more she could find. She drove home with her head spinning. Monday morning could not come quick enough.

Valerie Boothman

Chapter 19

Helen and John Moss were a young English couple who lived on a smallholding in St Lucy. Helen was a teacher at Harrison College teaching English and John imported computer parts. Their house was a single storey bungalow built on the top of a plateau in a very quiet and unspoilt part of the island. It was in many ways an unpopular area of the island but they loved it. They had a few chickens and a pig and a few goats tethered so they couldn't spoil the little bit of garden Helen had nurtured. The Mosses had invited Tom and Carrie Porter and Lucy to supper on Saturday evening. Lucy nearly declined as she was finding it very difficult to concentrate on anything but the newspaper articles she had read. Carrie reminded her to dress simply as Helen didn't like people to dress up. They rarely accepted invites to dine out and only occasionally invited special friends to supper. Lucy had been messing about during the day, she created more 'branches' to her family tree on 'Ancestry' and had a swim in the afternoon after the heat of the mid-day sun had passed. She showered and wrapped in her towel examined the contents of her wardrobe. She chose an old lilac coloured long straight sleeveless shift dress. She fingered the gold chain round her neck and chose a pair of small gold earrings. Lucy brushed her hair and decided it needed a cut next week. She slipped on a pair of white sandals and walked over to the long mirror. "What do you think Ben?" she asked out loud. "Oh I know I look just fine" she nodded. Then she added "I am going to have to concentrate tonight or my mind will be drifting away and I won't be listening to their conversation" then she laughed realising that she hadn't told Ben anything about her investigations - not yet!

Lucy heard the car, so quickly locked up and dropped the door keys into her bag. She often took them with her when she went out in the evening. As Tom drove away from Tamarind she was happy to be sitting in the back seat of his BMW not having to get too involved in their conversation. He drove along Highway 2 past Mullins Beach towards Speightstown, He turned right passing The Frangipani Art Gallery and The Sugar Cane Club up Mile and a Quarter hill. They were driving away from the expensive villas in St James. There were fewer houses now but several brightly coloured chattel houses and a few rum shops and you could hear loud Caribbean music being played. As they approached St Lucy Church Tom said "Not far now" and it coincided with Carrie saying "Nearly there" at the very same time. They all laughed. They passed an old broken sign on the side of the road where the letters MOSS could just about be identified. They turned down an old track over a few bumps in the road. Helen and John came out to meet them as Tom parked the car, and a few chickens ran to greet them too before Helen shooed them away. Lucy was warmly welcomed, she hadn't seen them since Ben's funeral so it was a poignant moment. John looked as though he hadn't changed clothes since breakfast and Helen wore denim shorts and a white tee shirt. She was wearing a brightly coloured necklace of pieces of wood. Lucy liked this couple.

Their house was quite isolated. It was desperately in need of a coat of paint and the verandah which circled the place needed repairing. Old cane furniture with huge cushions were positioned where you could sit and watch the sunrise

Valerie Boothman

and similar furniture was placed where you could watch the sun set. Helen motioned them to sit down as Tom emerged from the kitchen with a large glass jug of golden liquid and ice cubes and glasses saying "Rum punches everyone?" Lucy nodded and sank into the most wonderfully comfortable old chair, the stuffing was leaking but Lucy thought "if only this chair could talk". Helen bought the furniture at Charity Shops and Garage Sales and all she wanted was comfort for her and her guests. Their chairs were positioned in a crescent shape so they could all watch the sunset and yet conversation between them was easy. The night was still, there was a very slight warm breeze and there were just distant noises of the sea crashing on the rocks at North Point, insects buzzing round the light, and the soft animal noises from the goats and chickens. Lucy sipped her Rum Punch and felt very much at ease. The sun was setting and soon darkness would be all around them.

"I suppose it hasn't been easy for you without Ben" John Moss said suddenly. Lucy was taken aback "Well no it hasn't but I am lucky to have such good friends" as she pointed her hand towards Carrie and Tom. " Yes we have thought about you, it was so sudden" said Helen. For a while the conversation continued in this vein and sometimes they laughed about things they had all done together when Ben was alive. Lucy thought how sensible the Mosses were. Some people never mentioned Ben when they met her as if they thought she would get upset if they did. This was so much better, so natural. She didn't want them to forget him. Although the sun had now disappeared there was a strange light on the horizon, as though the sun was reluctant to leave them. They moved to the dining table next to where they were sitting and

John helped Helen to carry out a few large dishes of food. There was a huge bowl of salad, lettuce, peppers and thin slices of mango, a dish of sliced tomatoes in a vinaigrette dressing, a plate of pumpkin fritters and a platter of breaded flying fish. Helen carried a basket of her own baked bread "just break a bit off if you want some we don't bother with bread knives" she laughed. She aroma from the bread was heavenly and Lucy was glad she had skipped lunch. Later when their plates were empty Helen placed a cheese board on the table and John opened another bottle of wine.

The conversation ebbed and flowed, sometimes they just enjoyed the silence and the consciousness that they were amongst good friends. Helen looked across at her husband and smiled. She moved her fingers as though she was playing a guitar and nodded her head slightly. John stood up and went inside. Helen and Lucy cleared the table and placed the food in the kitchen as Carrie and Tom plumped up the cushions on the chairs and they all returned to where they had been sitting. John carried his Classical guitar and sat on a stool to one side of them. No one spoke as Helen refilled their glasses. John played a few chords and tuned his guitar as they all fell silent. He then started to play 'Romanza'. The long thin fingers of his left hand found the chords and the fingers of his right hand plucked the strings. The plaintiff melody pierced the air and drifted away from them yet created the most magical ambience. When he finished there was silence for several seconds before Helen said "Bravo" and smiled across to him. Everyone applauded with enthusiasm. "A pity no-one knows who composed it, I have a feeling they would have been very famous" John said. They all nodded. Everyone knew that the single performance should not be

Valerie Boothman

repeated. It was that special. They chatted for a while and then "Well we must leave you" said Tom, and they all rose slowly as though reluctant to leave the moment. Lucy hugged Helen and John and said nothing. There were tears in her eyes, and theirs, and words would have been superfluous. It was a quiet ride home to Tamarind but it was a very comfortable silence. Tom decided to wait until Lucy was in the house with all her lights on before he and Carrie drove home. Lucy walked through to the verandah, opening just one door and said to Ben "I have had a lovely evening sweetheart, you would have enjoyed it." Only the cicadas answered her so she closed the door and went to bed.

Chapter 20

On Monday morning at 10 am Lucy was sitting at a table in the Archives Record Office of Birth Marriages and Deaths in Old Lazarotte offices. She was looking for the birth record of Louise Balfour. It didn't take her long to find it.

Born: 28th August 1906 Fairfields Plantation House St Philip - Name: Louise Balfour, Sex: Girl, Name and surname of father: Daniel Balfour, Name and maiden name of mother: Rebecca Balfour, formerly Pilgrim, Occupation of father: Plantation owner, Signature, description and residence of informant: Daniel Balfour, father, Fairfields, When registered: 3rd September 1906, Signature of registrar: Jacob Braithwaite.

So Daniel Balfour was Louise Balfour's father.

Lucy obtained a copy and thanked the staff and then drove to the Barbados Advocate Archive offices. Now she thought she knew why Daniel Balfour had been angry. His daughter was Louise Balfour. She had to find another link, something to explain why he had challenged David Keppel. What was the name of the 16 year old boy who had been charged with rape. Was it David Keppel? If so was he held in custody prior to the trial? Why was he free? Before her was the microfilm reader and she was trying to find where she had stopped on Friday. She found it. The case had been adjourned so she was looking for where there was a report of the continuation of the trial, There it was on an inside page of the newspaper. She wondered if she had missed any earlier reports but at least she was now into the accounts of the trial. The reporter stated that the name of the victim was withheld due to her age. The Magistrates advised that the name of the accused should be withheld unless found guilty. This would protect any person accused but found innocent.

The reporter covered the important aspects of the trial. A party had taken place at The Marine Hotel to celebrate May Day. The party was held on the Saturday 3rd of May 1919 attended by plantation owners and their families and visitors from overseas but young men and women under the age of 18 years were not allowed to attend. Some sons and daughters had resented this and a group of them had decided to go to the hotel and hide somewhere and watch the fun. One youth had persuaded a young female person from a neighbouring plantation to join them. The boys took bottles of rum with them and had consumed a quantity by the time they arrived. The youth and the girl had become separated from the others and she became scared and wanted to go home. The youth tried to persuade her to stay but she ran away. He drank more rum and then decided he should try to find her. He found her in one of the outhouses attached to the hotel and struggled with her trying to persuade her to return to the hotel. In the struggle her dress was torn. The offence took place in the same building. Her screams were heard by partygoers who were sitting on the verandah. When they found her the youth had disappeared. The police found him the next day in an area near to his home.

The report went on to say that a youth had been arrested and pleaded guilty to the charge. The youth's father had originally challenged the charge and suggested that any one of the youths that night could have been responsible for the atrocity. The reporter did not give details of the questioning of the youth nor of the witnesses.

Lucy read the words, huge tears were hanging on her lower eyelids waiting to fall. She didn't need to read the details of the questioning. Her imagination took her to a warm night in May when a young girl had foolishly gone with a group of youths to watch the adults enjoying themselves at a glamorous party. The music would have been loud and the lights would be dazzling. She could imagine them peering through the windows, watching their parents drinking and dancing, peeping round corners, hoping not to be discovered. The girl would have enjoyed seeing all the ladies in their party dresses. Drinking rum would not have appealed to her but she would have noticed the effect it had on the boys. Lucy could imagine the girl becoming frightened and wanting to return to the safety of her home. A 16 year old boy struggling with her and tearing her dress would see the body of a young women. Any respect for her had gone due to his drunken state and in the darkness of an outbuilding he had committed an awful crime. In that moment an innocent girl had become a tool for drunken lust. Lucy looked for a tissue in her handbag. She sniffed and wiped away her tears. She wept for them both. The presiding Magistrate announced that sentence would be passed the next day.

Before she could read anymore Lucy went to get another drink of water and then returned to the desk. It was not difficult to find the next days report of the trial. She saw the heading " On the 10th May 1919 Guilty Verdict on Rape Case'. Lucy shivered. She read " In the Juvenile Justice Section of The Magistrates Court Bridgetown today Joshua Keppel age 16 years was found guilty of unlawful sex and rape of an underage girl in the Store Shed of The Marine Hotel on 3rd May 1919. The name of the victim was withheld due to her age. The Magistrates passed sentence after listening to a plea for leniency in respect of Mr Keppel's unblemished record and age. The Magistrates advised that Mr Keppel had pleaded guilty to the charge which had shown respect to the Court and under these circumstances the judiciary were allowed to use their discretion. Due to the plea of guilty the victim had been spared questioning by Council and a report signed by the victim had been admitted as evidence. Sentence was passed - two years in The Government Industrial School.

Chapter 21
1919

During the first week on board Edward was frequently sea sick and very weak and Charlotte too suffered from sea sickness. The Channel crossing to Cherbourg was smooth and they both enjoyed watching the ship entering the harbour and then leaving the French shore. The Ship's Doctor was very helpful and the Captain's wife helped Charlotte enormously. They became the best of friends and Charlotte was able to confide in her all her hopes and fears. Some of the other passengers were very agreeable and when Edward preferred to stay in their cabin Charlotte was able to socialise and enjoyed conversation whilst enjoying the sea breezes. During the second week Edward improved and Charlotte found him a corner of the deck where he was comfortable and she made sure he was well wrapped up when necessary.

In the afternoon of their fifteenth day when Charlotte had just settled Edward in his favourite corner on the deck there was a shout of 'land'. Although it was barely a smudge on the horizon everyone was excited even the crew. The Captain advised all the passengers that they would be docking in Bridgetown during the evening and would stay on board that night but would embark in the morning so make sure all their packing was ready for collection at early light. Their main luggage was stowed away but they had only been allowed minimum luggage in their cabins and Charlotte was looking forward to being on dry land with decent washing facilities and different clothes. She had brought lengths of materials with her, light cottons and linen which she hoped would be useful for a hot climate if she found a good dressmaker.

As Edward was so weak she had arranged for extra help with their luggage when they landed. All this was organised secretly to avoid embarrassment for Edward. Charlotte felt a huge confusion of excitement and trepidation as they were now so close to their new life. She prayed that the friend of her father in law Dr Stephen Drayton would be there to meet them. She prayed that he would be a gentleman and support them as was promised. Without his assistance this venture could be one huge mistake. Just what did Barbados hold for them? This little island twenty-one miles long and fourteen miles wide. Before she retired for the night she went up on deck, the smudge was now bigger. Under her breath she whispered 'Barbados'.

They had docked in Bridgetown during the night and all the passengers were ready for embarkation at an early hour. Charlotte stood with Edward looking down on the scene. The weather was very hot and they had both dressed in their summer clothes and Edward wore his Panama hat. Charlotte wore a straw bonnet and she pulled the front of it over her eyes as the bright sunlight nearly blinded her. She had never heard so much noise. The crew and Barbadians were swarming all over the decks hauling mail crates from the hold and stacking luggage ready for transferring to the dock. Charlotte could see quite a few well dressed people standing in the shade of the warehouses. It looked as though they were waiting for passengers. She hoped Dr Drayton was amongst them. Edward's father had given them a description of him. There was so much activity she wondered when they would receive instructions to move. Their cabin luggage had been collected hours earlier. The friends they had made on the voyage came up to them to say goodbye and promised they would meet again soon. Charlotte was worried that Edward would have difficulty transferring from ship to shore and hoped they would not be hurried. Suddenly she saw a horse and trap moving along the dock side. The driver was a tall gentleman wearing a straw hat and waving a red scarf. They both waved back and tears were streaming down Charlottes cheeks. Dr Drayton had arrived to welcome them to Barbados.

Chapter 22

Lucy drove home from Bridgetown. During the forty minute drive it was difficult to concentrate so much information was whirling around in her head. She parked the car. As she walked down the path to Tamarind for once she didn't notice the Frangipani, she didn't notice anything. She walked into the house and opened up the doors to the verandah and sat down.. She phoned Bailey Goodrich and Waters and made an appointment to see James the next day. At first the Receptionist said Mr Waters was unable to take any appointments until the following day but Lucy said "Please ask him?". When the Receptionist returned she was told that he would see her at 11am the next day. Lucy changed into her favourite baggy shorts and sloppy tee shirt and made some tea.

She carried through to the verandah a tray with her mothers best china teapot and cup and saucer to match. She leaned back in her chair and sipped her tea enjoying every drop. She thought "at such times you really can't beat a nice cup of tea". After her second cup she found her self closing her eyes and drifting into a deep sleep. Lucy woke suddenly to the sound of the telephone ringing. It was Alex, Rob's wife phoning from Perth but she was only asking how she was. "Oh dear" she thought, so many people are concerned for me, she knew her absences from the house, and visits into Bridgetown which she never liked to explain, made good friends wonder what she was doing. They cared for her and suspected the grieving process was having a strange effect on her. In actual fact all her investigating had helped to cope with grief. She still missed Ben, always would, but being on her own had given her the opportunity to investigate a mystery which had been at the back of her mind for years.

Lucy gathered together all the relative documents including her hand written copies of the newspaper reports. Tomorrow was a big day, no more guessing, she wanted facts from James Waters. She thought she would try to have an early night but doubted she would get much sleep.

She rose early and took an orange from the fruit basket. She peeled it and cut it into small chunks and placed it in a glass bowl. Then she washed a papaya and cut it in half. She scooped out the black seeds and placed them in her kitchen waste bin and peeled the fruit. She cut the flesh into pieces and added them to the orange and gently stirred it. She spooned a good helping into a small bowl and put the rest in the fridge saying to herself "enough for two more breakfasts, that will keep me going" and couldn't help but laugh at the double meaning. She sat on the verandah eating her breakfast and wondered what the day held for her.

Of course Lucy was early and had to wait several minutes before James Waters could see her. When they were sitting in his office and she was facing him across the dark red leather topped desk he looked at her quizzically. She smiled at him. "What have you found?" he said and smiled. She said nothing but she spread all her documents in front of him. He studied them and read her copies of the newspaper reports and then looked up and stared at her. Lucy said "James, I believe my mother was born on 10th February 1920. On that date a child was born in

Barbados named Louise, the daughter of Louise Balfour but no fathers name is recorded on her birth certificate. I know that the rape of a young girl took place nine months earlier in May 1919. I also know a Daniel Balfour was accused of threatening and angry behaviour to David Keppel." Lucy repeated the name "Daniel Balfour" She continued "As you can see from my documents I know that a Joshua Keppel was convicted of the rape of a young girl. That girls name was withheld. My family had held in safe keeping a receipt for services by your company dated 28th February 1920 the date Louise Balfour registered the birth of her daughter" James stared at her but she continued. "James do I need to say more? I know you have information and the time has come for you to enlighten me".

She slowly gathered her documents and placed them in her brown manila file. She grasped her hands together, she felt quite calm, and then she looked up at him. James coughed nervously and said "I think we need a cup of tea" and phoned through to his Secretary. James elbows were on the desk and he rested his chin on his hands, staring at Lucy whilst they waited. Lucy sipped her tea and felt remarkably calm "whatever he was going to tell her was better than not knowing" she thought.

James phoned through to his Secretary and said they must not be disturbed under any circumstances. That's when Lucy started to feel nervous. "Well Lucy" he started. "Some of what I now tell you may not be strictly correct or true. I can only tell you what I believe to be the truth and that is why I needed you to find out as much as you could from other sources". Lucy nodded her head. James Waters continued " You are aware of the rape case but what was withheld from the press reports was the age of the girl. Louise Balfour was only 14 years old when she was raped and was 15 when she gave birth." Lucy flinched, this was worse than she had imagined. " As a result of that heinous act Louise Balfour gave birth to a daughter on 10th February 1920. When her father discovered that she was with child (as a result of the rape) he was demented and vowed that he would not support the bastard child of Joshua Keppel who was then serving his sentence in the Government Industrial School. Louise at that time was ill and under the care of Doctor Stephen Drayton." Lucy shook her head in dismay.

James continued "Daniel Balfour, the father of Louise, was adamant that the child must be adopted. Remember Louise was only 15 years old when the child was born. Louise was worried that her father would harm the child. Daniel Balfour asked Doctor Drayton to find a couple who would adopt the child when it was born. You are aware that your grandfather James Richards had served in World War 1 and had been discharged through sickness. He was not a well man and his father arranged for him and his wife, your grandmother Charlotte, to winter in Barbados during the 1919/1920 winter. They left Southampton aboard a Royal Mail Steam Packet ship and during their long stay here Dr Drayton attended your grandfather for his ailments. Your grandmother told Dr Drayton that she was now aged thirty and had been told there was little possibility that they would have children". James Waters stopped speaking and poured them both another cup of tea.

"I trust you can see where this is leading, Lucy?" he said. She nodded and he continued. "Louise Balfour agreed to the adoption of her baby although at her age she really had no say in the matter. She could not have supported herself never mind a baby. However, her father insisted that the Richards must agree that the child would never return to the island. They agreed. Louise gave birth to her daughter at her home, Fairfields in St Philips and Dr Drayton attended her. She refused to give the fathers name on the Birth Certificate although it was not a mystery. My grandfather, Lionel Waters, drew up an adoption agreement having carried out a limited search that your grandparents were able to support the child". James then opened a drawer in his desk and placed a file in front of Lucy. From the file he withdrew a white paper, yellowed at the corners, and turned it so that Lucy could read it. The paper bore the letter heading of Goodrich and Waters. Beneath the words of the agreement, it bore the signatures of Charlotte and James Richards. On the next line was the childish scrawl of Louise Balfour. Her age was stated as 15 years. At the foot of the paper was the signature of Lionel Waters, and the date, 28th February 1920. It was too much for Lucy to bear when she saw the childish handwriting of Louise Balfour. She was signing away her child. Lucy pulled herself together. "So the baby was my mother and Louise Balfour was my grandmother" she said. James nodded.

"Obviously your grandmother Charlotte named the baby Susan but kept the name her real mother had given to her. I cannot fill in all the gaps in this story" said James. "I don't know the date they left Barbados. I don't know if they ever disclosed to their relations in England that they had adopted a child. You must think that your grandmother eventually told your mother of the circumstances of her birth" James said. "She must have done" Lucy said "which is why she never returned to the island, they kept their promise". James said "It is your decision if you wish to carry out more research, but I can't help you anymore". He pushed the file containing the adoption agreement across to Lucy "this is yours" he said "we should by rights have destroyed it long ago" he added. "Glad you didn't" Lucy said.

Lucy looked at James Waters " I am so glad I chose to come to you with my problems" she said. "Well actually, me too" James added as he opened the door for her "it has been a real pleasure, I am sorry I couldn't have been more helpful in the early stages. I had to put pressure on my father to remember what his father had told him. This island is so small I am sure we will be bumping into each other again". Just as she was leaving James added "Oh just one more thing, I believe Louise died when she was still a young women, she never married, I believe she never really recovered." Lucy nodded and raised her hand as a goodbye, stunned by the news that her grandmother had never had more family. "Poor girl" she said quietly to herself. James went with her to the door and watched her walk away down the street.

Chapter 23

Driving home to Tamarind Lucy considered all the facts. She was weary of her search but knew an inner peace. Who had known that Charlotte and James Richards had adopted a baby? Does it really matter, she thought. Her quest had been to find out why her mother would not come to Barbados, now she knew why. She would phone Carrie when she got back to Tamarind. She should be the first person she told, it would explain her behaviour and absences during the last few months. It started to rain as she drove home and it was raining heavily when she pulled off the road behind Tamarind. She took off her smart sandals and ran barefoot down the path. She found the key and struggled trying to keep her folder dry whilst turning the lock. She nearly ran to the phone shaking her wet hair and phoned Carrie. "Oh good you are there, can you come down, I have lots to tell you" she said. Carrie recognised the urgency in Lucy's voice and agreed to drop everything.

The rain had stopped but the verandah was wet and so they sat at her kitchen table with two cups of coffee. Lucy started at the beginning explaining the reason for her wishing to solve the mystery. Once she began there was no stopping her. Carrie stared at her saying nothing. Lucy explained all her visits to the Solicitors and her searches at The Advocate Archive offices. She showed Carrie the birth certificates, her grandfather's discharge certificate from the army, everything. She stopped once to make some fresh coffee. Carrie was a very good listener. Eventually she showed Carrie the adoption agreement. "That young man raped my real grandmother, a girl of 14 years, just imagine it. He probably never served two years. He was then free to live a normal life." Carrie looked at Lucy "What is there left for you to do" she asked in a very quiet voice. Lucy said "Well I am content now, I understand why Louise asked that her baby should never return. She was protecting her. I can imagine the joy the baby gave to my grandparents who could not have children. I am pleased that my grandmother kept the name her baby's real mother had given her although it must have always reminded her of Louise Balfour". Suddenly Lucy looked very sad. "What's the matter?" asked Carrie. "I want to find Louise's grave, that's the only thing I want to do" Lucy said.

Carrie picked up her car keys. Lucy looked at her. "Come on lets go, there is plenty of time before sunset" Carrie said. Lucy quickly locked the cottage and climbed into the passenger seat of Carrie's car. "Where are we going?" she asked. "We will try St Johns church first" Carrie answered "that's where your mother was baptised". Lucy felt rather confused and they sat in silence on the way there. Carrie parked the car and took Lucy's hand. They walked beneath the tall trees and Carrie led Lucy down a narrow path passing several gravestones until they arrived at a narrow grave. Lucy stared at the grave, then she knelt down. The inscription read 'Louise Balfour 1906 - 1922 - At peace'.

Lucy stroked the letters on the stone and pulled some weeds away from the grave. She was puzzled. She looked up at Carrie whose face was as white as stone. "You knew" Lucy exclaimed "You knew where her grave was, you knew Carrie" disbelief in her voice. She remained kneeling looking up at Carrie's ashen face. Carrie spoke very quietly "You are going to hate me Lucy". Carrie looked away, her shoulders slumped and then turned back to meet Lucy's gaze. She hesitated for a long time before continuing " my mother's maiden name was Keppel - she was Margaret Keppel when she married my father, my grandfather was Joshua Keppel".

Lucy listened to the words and shook her head very slowly. Carrie turned away and began walking back towards the Church. Lucy watched her go. She saw Carrie enter the Church. Lucy turned to the grave, she tended the grave as best she could her tears falling on the stone making dark grey blotches. It was the grave of a sixteen year old girl.

Lucy slowly walked away from the grave, along the path towards the Church. She entered the Church and saw Carrie sitting in a pew on the left hand side, half way down. Lucy walked down the side isle and sat next to her. She sat for several minutes then opened a Book of Common Prayer. Inside was a white card with black edging. The embossed words read "You shall not bow yourself down to them, nor serve them, for I the LORD your God am a jealous God, visiting the iniquity of the fathers upon the sons to the third and fourth generation of those that hate Me, and doing mercy to thousands of those who love Me and keep My commandments - Deuteronomy Chapter 5."

Carrie's head was in her hands and she was weeping. Lucy took her hand and guided her out of church. "Enough tears" said Lucy, "you have had enough to bear" and she put her arms around her and hugged her.

They drove back to Tamarind, Carrie said she wouldn't come in she preferred to go home and talk to Tom. Lucy understood and suggested that perhaps tomorrow they could meet up for a coffee. Carrie put her arm round Lucy's shoulders and smiled "you seem to be at peace" then she left. Lucy watched her walk up the path and climb into her car and drive away. She thought of the words Carrie had used "at peace" the same words engraved on Louise Balfour's grave.

Lucy knew she would not be leaving Barbados. She would email the Bennetts and suggest they made her an offer on the house in England. She would visit Rob and his family sometime, but it would be just that, a visit. Tomorrow she would put flowers on Louise Balfour's grave and may take a walk along Cattlewash and she would visit Carrie, the woman who shared the same grandfather. Lucy shivered.

Lucy kicked off her sandals. She walked towards the kitchen. She opened the cupboard and took down a tall slim glass with a heavy base from the shelf. She added the gin and three ice cubes from the freezer compartment of her fridge. She cut a slice of lime and added it to the glass. She poured the tonic water until it was about an inch from the rim and watched the bubbles climb the sides of the glass.

Gently lifting it to her ear she shook the glass, she could hear the cubes clinking. Lucy walked towards the verandah, she sat down carefully in her swing chair and pushed her bare feet against the wooden floor so that the chair swung to and fro. She looked out towards the sea and looked down into the garden at the huge red blossoms

---

of the Hibiscus. She looked through the branches of the Mahogany trees where sun was filtering through, creating stripes of shade and sun on the verandah. She lifted the glass to her lips allowing the liquid to cool her throat. Lucy took another sip and said "Now Ben, have I got a story to tell you?"

33564758R00068

Printed in Great Britain
by Amazon